TODD CAMPBELL

The Everyday Adventurer Series - Think Like a Wizard

Master your mind. Shape your reality. Become the spellcaster of your own life.

A Word From the Author

This book draws inspiration from the realms of fantasy and the challenges of real life. While references to roleplaying concepts are used metaphorically, all content is independently created and unaffiliated with any specific companies or brands.

The stories and reflections within are based on lived experience and personal insight. I offer them in the spirit of growth, wonder, and shared adventure.

First edition

ISBN: 9798316409198

Cover art by Shelly Fierro

This book was professionally typeset on Reedsy.
Find out more at reedsy.com

Contents

About The Series

The Everyday Adventurer is a series of motivational books inspired by the legendary fantasy classes found in tabletop role-playing games.

Each volume focuses on a different archetype, not as escapism, but as a lens for real-life transformation. Classes give us a framework. They help us see ourselves not as broken or behind, but simply untrained. They remind us that we can grow, that we can evolve., that we have choices. Whether you're drawn to the wisdom of the Wizard, the charm of the Bard, the discipline of the Monk, or the courage of the Paladin, each class reflects a unique part of who we are and who we could become.

These aren't books about playing a game.

They're about playing *life* differently.

Each chapter blends genuine stories, science, rituals, and reflection, designed to help you level up in your own world.

This first book begins with the Wizard:

The learner.
The seeker.

The one who believes that knowledge, curiosity, and imagination can shape reality. Your class is just the beginning. Your adventure is already underway.

The path begins with the Wizard... but every class reveals a different truth.
Follow them all and discover who you were meant to be.

How To Use This Book

This isn't a book you read once and forget. It's a spellbook.

That means you don't just consume it, you interact with it. You write in the margins. You pause mid-chapter to journal. You try things. You cast minor spells. You fail sometimes. Then you come back stronger.

This book is meant to be:

- Read in a way that matches your current energy - slowly or in sprints.
- Used as a personal guide, not a rigid curriculum.
- Returned to as you grow, change, and revisit old spells with fresh eyes.

Each chapter is designed to offer:

- A story or insight to reframe how you think.
- A lesson or principle from the Wizard's path.
- A quest or ritual you can try in real life. Small, flexible, and powerful over time.

Some chapters might hit harder than others. That's okay. You're not here to master everything at once. You're here to become the kind of person who keeps learning.

Tip: Start a journal, doc, or Notion page for your Wizard's Spellbook. Capture your thoughts, quotes, failed spells, breakthrough moments, and experiments. This is your grimoire. Let it evolve with you.

Reading Paths

- **First time through?** Start at the beginning. Let the journey unfold.
- **Feeling stuck in life?** Flip to the part that matches your current challenge. That's the section you need right now.
- **Need a quick hit of insight?** Open a random page. Let the book surprise you.

You don't need to finish to get value. You just need to begin.

A Note on the Codex

Throughout the book, you'll see words like "mana," "ritual," "spellbook," and "casting." These are metaphors, not mechanics. But if you ever feel lost, flip to **The Wizard's Codex** for quick definitions.

This book isn't about pretending to be a wizard. It's about remembering that you've always been one.

Let's begin.

Introduction

I grew up loving fantasy worlds filled with danger, wonder, monsters, and magic. It wasn't just the battles or the treasure. I was drawn to the characters, the classes, the roles. Not just who they were, but how they lived. Every class was different, but they all had something in common: each one made a choice. A choice to grow, to take action, to push beyond comfort and step into something bigger than themselves. And somewhere along the way, I realized that life isn't all that different.

We may not have dragons, but we face fear. We may not cast spells, but we shape reality with our choices. We may not roll dice for every decision, but chance, risk, and timing are always in play. You don't have to be the strongest, fastest, or flashiest. You just need to choose the life you want and build the character who lives it.

You don't have to escape reality to become an adventurer. You just need to start playing the game differently.

The Wizard's Path

You don't need a tower, a wand, or a glowing staff.

To be a Wizard in this life, all you need is a question and the courage to follow where it leads.

This book is your grimoire: a space to wonder, to write, to remember who you are and who you're becoming.

The spells are simple. The rituals are small. But the results?

Transformative.

Welcome to the Wizard's path.

I

The Apprentice

Every Wizard starts as uncertain, curious, and untested. This part is about saying yes to the path, even before you feel ready. It's about trading perfection for progress, embracing the unknown, and daring to believe you're meant for more. Before you master your magic. You have to choose to show up, again and again. This is where your journey begins.

The robe doesn't make the wizard. The choice to begin does.

The Call to Learn

> **"The ones who rise are rarely chosen. They're the ones who choose themselves."**
> — *The Unknown Archmage*

The Whisper of More

Every great story starts with a whisper.

A quiet voice asking, *Is this it?*
A flicker of discomfort.
Not a shout or dramatic event.

A deeper knowing, the kind that stirs inside you and whispers. There's more.

For me, that whisper came in the still moments. The spaces between work, bills, errands, and sleep. When the noise of life faded just enough for a question to slip through.

What do I want to leave behind?

That question keeps coming back. It got louder after I lost both of my parents, just a few years apart. They hadn't been together in a long time. I loved them both deeply, and they both loved me.

My mom and I talked on the phone nearly every day. Even when we weren't in the same place, her voice was a constant in my life. She believed in everything I did. Losing her was like a light going out in a room I didn't realize was lit.

My dad, the man who taught me guitar, wasn't always around. Our relationship had gaps, but we still talked. He still showed up. When he passed, it hit in ways I didn't expect. It created silence in places I thought were full.

His absence reminded me of something simple and heavy: life is finite. We don't have centuries. We don't respawn. Our time is short. So I asked myself: What am I doing with that time? What am I building? What will I leave behind when my time is up?

That thought stuck. Not with a clear map or grand revelation. It arrived like a pull. A quiet invitation. To write, to speak. To turn my inner stories into something useful, something *real*. Something that might actually help someone else.

That's when I realized I didn't just want more.

I wanted meaning.

The Spark: A Kid with Questions

I've always loved learning, even as a kid. I was the one asking "why" a dozen times too many. I wasn't trying to be annoying, but because I really wanted to know.

One memory sticks with me like a glowing rune in my personal spellbook. When I was young, a repairman came to fix our dishwasher. Most kids would've gone back to watching cartoons or playing outside, but not me. I parked myself nearby and watched like it was a magic show. It was mesmerizing, every screw, every movement. Like the world was unfolding, one part at a time.

After that, my mom encouraged me. "Always ask questions," she'd say. "Look for the 'whys.'"

She had that same wonder about the world. I know I got that spark from her, not the dishwasher, but her.

That spark never went out. It got louder in books, comics, games, and fantasy stories. They gave me language for things I didn't know how to say yet.

One of my favorite books is *The Name of the Wind*. It's about a hero who isn't really a hero. That hit home, because most of us don't feel powerful or legendary.

We just feel like us, but we still want something *more*.

The Struggle with Feeling "Average"

Most of my life, I felt average.

I wasn't the strongest, the fastest, or the smartest. I was trying… not the top of the class, but trying. They didn't vote me "Most Likely to Succeed." Yeah, it bothered me sometimes.

Even when I felt behind, I kept showing up. If I would not be the best, fine. I'd be the one who keeps going.

Growing up, I thought smart people had the answers. They seemed to have received some secret manual that I never got. Success looked polished.

Instagram-filtered.

Perfect house—Check
Perfect job—Check
Perfect smile—Check
That wasn't real, it was the *illusion.*

Now I look around at my life and realize. I do have the perfect house. It's not flawless, but it's mine. Same with my family and with my work. They're not magazine perfect, but they're mine. That's a kind of success no one else can define for me. I still feel behind sometimes, but I'm not stuck there anymore. I'm not stuck in the cycle of wishing for something that isn't real.

Turning Rejection into a Spell

A while back, I applied for a data analyst job. I made it through three rounds of interviews, I was a finalist; I was sure I had it.

Then two weeks passed, and nothing. Radio silence.

I followed up. They picked someone else, and it stung. I asked all the usual questions.

What did I do wrong?
What didn't I have?

Instead of spiraling, I shifted. I told myself, next time, they won't have a reason to pass. So I started learning. It wasn't out of panic, but out of purpose. I dove into advanced data methods; I stacked skills; I studied at night. I turned the rejection into a new incantation.

Because I knew this: **Growth is the only way forward.**

Learning Like Me

For me, learning has always been slow, stubborn, and a bit messy.

But also… kind of magic.

Like when I tried to learn viola in fifth grade. The sheet music made little sense to me, everyone else seemed to get it, but I didn't. The teacher gave up early, but I didn't give up on myself. I treated the viola like a guitar, I plucked notes one by one. Matched what I heard; Mistake by mistake. It wasn't about passing the class; it was about figuring it out *my* way. I stayed up late practicing, rewinding the same piece over and over until it felt right.

I didn't bring sheet music to the school competition, just my instrument. I played the Star Wars theme, my mom's favorite, and walked out with a first-place ribbon.

It wasn't because I learned like everyone else. It was because I learned like me. That changed something in me. It rewired how I saw myself.

Learning isn't about doing it "their" way. It's about finding the path that makes sense to *you*.

That same approach stuck with me when I learned to code. I'd break things down like music, like spells . When I stopped asking:

Why can't I get this?
How does this make sense to me?

That's when everything changed and learning stopped being schoolwork.

It became **spellwork**.

Owning the Wizard Path

Most people would say I'm a Bard.

Music? Check.
Charisma? Usually.
Quick with words? Absolutely.

I've spent time in that archetype, but it never fully fit. Because when you strip it all away, I'm not drawn to performance. I'm drawn to understanding.

I'm a Wizard.

I want to know how things work. Why systems behave the way they do. How to turn knowledge into change. Wizards study and they prepare spells. They dig under the surface to see what others miss and then they shape the world with what they've found. That's what I do.

Every day.

My version of spell prep? Reading, journaling, watching and studying. I keep a digital spellbook in Notion. I revisit it when I need to cast something new. I listen to people smarter than me and I track my questions. I let ideas stew before I cast them. I'm not trying to be the smartest person in the room. I'm just trying to see the room more clearly.

And that's what Wizards do.

Even my wife is a Wizard in her own way. When our AC broke, she didn't panic. She opened the panel, studied the system, and diagnosed the issue.

Compressor. Fixed. Done. Now that's wizardry.

Not just learning, but understanding. Not just knowing, but applying.

Wizards aren't flashy, and they aren't loud, but they're powerful. This is because they ask the right questions. They learn not just for the knowledge, but for change.

The Final Spell

The blank page isn't your enemy.

It's your ally.

It's the part of you that still believes anything is possible, and it's waiting. Not for perfection, but for presence. Every line you write, every question you ask, every messy first draft... is a spell of becoming.

Wizards aren't born.

They're written. One page at a time.

Apprentice Spell: Answer the Call

Choose one of the following to build your personal spellbook:

- **Name Your Spellbook** — Give your journal or doc a name that feels like yours. Make it official. This is your arcane archive now.
- **Write Your Wizard's Creed** — A few lines that ground you. What do you believe about growth? About learning? About your role as a Wizard in training?
- **Pick One Spell to Learn** — Not a goal. A spell. Something small and specific you want to study, understand, or try just because it calls to you.

Then, just begin. Even if it's messy, especially if it's messy.

The page becomes magic because you showed up.

The Blank Spellbook

"Do not fear the empty page. It is the only place real magic begins."
— *The Unknown Archmage*

The Blank Page as Power

A Wizard doesn't fear an empty spellbook.

They don't see it as failure or proof of being behind. They see it as sacred, a canvas of infinite possibility. The blank page isn't a void, it's unshaped magic. Potential, untouched by the pressure or perfection. Most people are terrified of starting from scratch and we're taught that blank means "nothing," and nothing means "not enough." But Wizards see it differently.

To a Wizard, the first page isn't something to avoid, it's something to honor. If the page is blank, it doesn't mean you've failed. It just means you haven't cast your first spell yet. This means you're still in the most powerful place of all. You are at the beginning.

This is where everything becomes possible. Where you can try, stumble, rewrite, and reshape. Past attempts don't limit your voice, you discover it in real time.

You don't need experience to begin and you don't need credentials to be curious. You just need the willingness to turn the page and write anyway. The world might say you're too late or that you need a full plan, more time. But Wizards know the truth. The page doesn't wait for you to be ready. It becomes ready because you begin.

So go ahead. Open the book, let the ink flow, write the first line. Even if it's messy, even if it's unsure. That first spell doesn't have to be perfect.

It just has to be yours.

A Spellbook With No Spells (Yet)

Before my spellbook lived in the cloud, it lived in my hands. Spiral-bound, creased at the corners, pages dog-eared and ink-stained. I always carried a notebook. Not for school, and no not for work. Just... for thoughts.

Things like quotes I liked, lines from anime, and random questions that hit me at stoplights or between shifts.

Sometimes, I'd hear a line in a show or story that lit something up in my brain. I'd scribble it down before it vanished, not to collect it, but to think about it. To turn it over and let it open doors in my mind.

I remember watching *Dragon Ball Z* as a kid. The main character of the show, Goku was training in a gravity chamber. This chamber could change the gravity to be heavier than whatever planet he was currently on. It looked cool, but something stuck. Could that actually work? What would happen if humans trained under higher gravity? So I wrote it down and later that day I started researching. That one question pulled me from anime into astronomy. From cartoons into planetary mass and resistance training. We can't crank up gravity in our backyards, but we can add resistance. And it works. Just like Goku. Just like magic.

That was the day I realized, learning isn't something you wait to be taught. That it's something you chase. That was one of the first spells I ever cast. I didn't know it then. I didn't have a syllabus, and I didn't need permission. I just needed a notebook, a question, and a willingness to wonder.

That curiosity never left. The notebooks became Google Docs, then Notion pages. Now I carry a digital grimoire filled with thoughts, insights, and experiments.

But it all started with a kid, a cartoon, and a question.

Zero to Something: The Day I Changed My Class

I never set out to become a coder, or an analyst, or anything in tech, really.

For a long time, I was just trying to find my way through the world. One odd job at a time. I've worked in call centers, collected debt, cleaned pools. At one point, I was even a preschool teacher.

A Jack of all trades.

Not because I couldn't commit, but because I wanted to learn. I wanted to see the world from every angle. Then 2020 hit. I was working as a customer service and sales agent. I started tinkering with Excel, specifically with VBA, and built a simple tool to access product info faster on calls.

Someone took notice of what I was creating. A lead on the website team pulled me aside and said, "I think you've got something here. Want to try building on our website with me?" I didn't know HTML, CSS, or JavaScript. I mean, I dabbled with MySpace back in the day, but I really didn't know any of it.

But I said yes.

And that single yes rewrote everything. I dove into tutorials, books, YouTube. I broke things, then I fixed them. Stayed up late troubleshooting code I didn't understand yet. It was slow, and it was frustrating. But also electric. I wasn't just learning a skill. I was rewriting my story.

Now, a few years later, I am still working with that team. I expanded into analytics, pulling data, understanding systems, and spotting patterns. What started with a spreadsheet turned into a full class change. I didn't level up. I multiclassed.

That first line of code? That was my arcane focus.

That moment didn't just teach me a new job. It taught me this, that starting from zero is where all true Wizards begin.

The Unfinished Stories That Taught Me Everything

I've always tried to write. I wrote stories, worlds, characters and plots. I'd pick up a notebook and dive in, but most of the time, I'd stop halfway. Not because I didn't care, but because something stopped clicking.

I'd hit a wall.
Lose the thread.

I would think, *Maybe I'm not meant to finish this.*

But I couldn't let the stories go. So I turned them into something else. I used them as the foundation for tabletop RPG campaigns. What I couldn't finish alone, I finished with others.

My half-built ideas became quests, characters, lore. We created something together. A living spell none of us could have written alone. I learned from those games that magic isn't always a solo act, that some spells are born in connection. Years later, when I finally finished my first book, *From an NPC to a Hero*, everything clicked. I never released that book, but it was the first one I actually finished.

I realized I didn't need to force the story, that I just had to write what was true to me.

That book became a finished spell in my grimoire. Just this one will be too.

The Lie of Being Behind

"You're not behind. You're just early in your journey."

That's what no one tells you when you're staring at someone else's highlight reel, wondering why your spellbook still feels empty. Comparison is a thief, and what it steals is clarity. It convinces you that you're late, you're not good enough, or that someone else's pace is the standard.

But you're not behind. You're just not on their path and you never were.

Wizards don't all study at the same pace. Some master fire spells early, some spend years in silence, while others fill their books slowly, with careful ink. On the other hand, some burn through scrolls and start over time and time again. There's no timeline for becoming who you are. Every Archmage was once a beginner with a blank book and trembling hands.

They weren't behind; they were just beginning, just like you.

So stop measuring your progress against someone else's magic, your spellbook isn't supposed to look like theirs.

It's supposed to look like you.

The Power of Beginner's Magic

There's something special about being new. You don't know the "rules" yet, which means you're not bound by them. You ask questions others stopped asking long ago and you try ideas that experienced minds might dismiss.

That's beginner's magic.
It's seeing with fresh eyes.
Trying before doubting.
Creating before second-guessing.

I remember the first time I played Dungeons & Dragons. I thought I'd be a natural. I'd read fantasy, and I knew all the tropes. Turns out, however, I didn't know a thing. There were rules, mechanics, collaboration, and conflict. Entire systems I didn't understand.

My friend Ken was our Dungeon Master, and he taught me everything I know. How to think like a player, how to engage with the world, how to adapt. The more I played, the more I noticed cracks in his system. Not in the game, but in how it could evolve. Ken's style had left space, and I stepped into it. So I started running my own games. Were they perfect? Not at all, but they were mine, and that made them magical.

I wasn't trying to be a rulebook.

I was trying to create a world where people could choose, explore, grow, and every time I sat behind the screen, I got better. Not because I mastered the mechanics, but because I remembered what it felt like to be new. I used that feeling to make sure my players felt like their choices mattered.

Beginner's magic doesn't just show up in games. It shows up in real life, too.

When I was a teenager, I thought I had everything figured out. Let's be honest, most of us do at that age. I'd worked all the typical mall jobs. Food court, toy store, even some random part-time roles. Then a friend convinced me to apply for a kiosk job selling turtles.

Yes. Turtles.

I knew nothing about turtles and even less about sales. But I was curious. That curiosity turned into one of the most important lessons I've ever learned. That job taught me how to interact with people. Not from a script, but from rhythm, from observation, from flow. I started noticing how people moved, how they spoke, how they reacted. I learned to mirror them, not to manipulate, but to connect. To make someone feel seen, understood, and safe.

I thought I was leveling up my Bard skills. But really, I was just collecting spells.

The kind you don't learn in a classroom. The kind that only show up when you're dropped into the unknown and say, "*Okay, let's see what I can learn from this.*"

Beginner's magic isn't about being the best. It's about being open. It's the courage to say:

I don't know this yet, but I'm willing to try.

Within that space, in that awkward, exciting, uncertain beginning, some of the most powerful spells are written.

Small Rituals for New Starts

A Wizard doesn't cast spells on impulse, they prepare. Not to be perfect, but to be present. They build rituals. Small, intentional acts that anchor them to the life they're trying to create. Because even the most powerful magic begins with a simple gesture.

Like opening a book, lighting the candle, and writing that first line.

When the spellbook is still blank, rituals make it real.

Why do rituals matter? Remember, rituals aren't rules, they're reminders. They tell your brain, *"This matters. This is part of who I am now."*

You don't need a robe or incense. You don't need a tower. What you need is rhythm. Something small and yours that says *I am a Wizard. I show up for my magic.*

Apprentice Spell: Your First Rituals

Think of these as your cantrips. Easy to cast but powerful.

1. Create Your First Page
Title your spellbook and give it some identity. It can be digital or physical, that doesn't matter. What matters is that you name it. Here are some ideas:

- *Field Notes of a Modern Wizard*
- *Experiments in Becoming*
- *Stuff I'm Learning Because I Refuse to Stay Stuck*

Open a doc, open a notebook, whatever works best for you. Name the page or even name yourself.

Just start it. That's the spell.

2. Write a Wizard's Creed
This isn't a goal or a mantra. It's a declaration.

Write 3–5 lines you can return to when you doubt yourself. Words that pull you back to who you're choosing to become.

For example:

- I do not fear the blank page. I create from it.
- I am not behind. I am becoming.
- I am a student of the world and a writer of my magic.
- I learn by failing. I grow by trying again.

Write your own. Speak it. Pin it somewhere.

Say it before casting a hard spell, like learning something new or trusting yourself again.

3. Name Your First Spell
Learning is magic. But it doesn't feel like magic when it's vague. So give your curiosity a name. Give your goal a form. Not something like, get better at stuff or fix my life.

But something like:

- *Understand the basics of SQL*
- *Get curious about why I freeze in meetings*
- *Create one blog post I'm proud of*
- *Figure out why I avoid journaling*

You name the spell.

And once it has a name, you can learn how to cast it.

A Ritual of Your Own

Want to build your own? Start with these prompts:

- What do I want to feel more of?
- What am I afraid to start but drawn toward anyway?
- What 5-minute ritual could honor that direction?

You don't need to meditate for an hour. You don't need a productivity system. You just need a reason to show up and a minor act that says:

I'm here. I'm learning. This matters.

My Ritual? It's Writing This.

This book is my ritual.

Every chapter is me casting something I used to keep hidden. Every page is a reminder that I'm still learning, still building, still becoming. Some days, my ritual is journaling, or it's a quote that hits like lightning. Some days it's walking and letting my mind wander. But no matter the form, the message is the same. You don't need to be ready.

You just need to begin.

Not Born With It

> **"The wisest Wizards don't hoard knowledge. They get excited when they realize how much they still don't know."**
> —*The Unknown Archmage*

The Myth of the Gifted Mage

Some people think Wizards are born with glowing eyes and ancient knowledge in their veins. That the moment they pick up a staff, they just *know,* as if the arcane were waiting for them to arrive.

The truth is…that's not how it works.

Experienced Wizards don't stumble into mastery. They build it, one spell at a time. If you peeked into the tower of a true Archmage, you wouldn't see divine talent carved into stone. You'd see thousands of failed rituals, burned pages, miscast spells and notes scribbled in the margins of old tomes. The real magic wasn't in their blood, it was in their persistence.

There's a lie we've all been told. That some people just "have it". That magic is in your DNA… or it isn't.

Experienced Wizards know better.

Power comes from study.
Growth comes from repetition.
Mastery comes from failing forward.

This chapter is for every apprentice who thought they didn't have what it takes, because the truth is, no one does... at first.

Why Talent Is Overrated

We love the idea of prodigies, those that just "get it". Our perception is there is no learning curve, no awkward phase, just instant excellence. It's a comforting fantasy and we attribute our struggles to their natural talent. It gives us an out, but the truth is less glamorous and way more powerful.

We build skill. Period.

Even research backs it up. Decades of psychological studies show that what we call talent is often just early exposure, consistent effort, and deliberate practice. Natural ability might give someone a head start.

But it won't take them across the finish line.

My Struggle With Feeling "Behind"

There were times I looked around and thought, *How are they so far ahead?* I'd watch someone explain a concept effortlessly, solve a complex problem in seconds, or create something brilliant on their first try.

Meanwhile, I was still stuck on step one.

It felt like I was the only one who had to try *this hard* to get it. When something took me longer than it took someone else, I assumed the worst.

I'm just not built for this.

But the truth is, I *was* building something. I just couldn't see it yet.

All the trials.
All the repetition.
All the time it took me to "finally" get it?

That was the training. That was the spellwork. The mistake wasn't in struggling; the mistake was thinking struggling meant I wasn't good enough.

Learning Like a Wizard

Here's what no one tells you: the best learners aren't fast.

They're curious.

They don't obsess over being perfect; they obsess over *understanding*. A Wizard doesn't look at a failed spell and say, "I must be broken." They ask themselves, "Okay, what went wrong?".

They study the ashes.
They tweak the incantation.
They try again.

That mindset makes them powerful. It's not speed, style, or some innate ability that you lack.

It's the willingness to stay in the lab when the spell won't fire.

The Danger of the "Effortless" Illusion

We only see the highlight reel, the polished work, or the confident presentation. We don't see is the backstory, the failed drafts, the nights of doubt and the hours of frustration. So we assume we're the only one fumbling through it.

We're not.

Every Wizard you admire? They have a shelf full of failures you've never seen. The more you chase effortlessness, the more you'll resent your own process. Real learning is messy. It's non-linear, and it's full of wrong turns.

But that doesn't make you broken. It makes you real.

No One Is Born Knowing Magic

They learn it, one spell at a time.

There's a myth that haunts both Wizards and learners alike. It's the belief that some people are just gifted. That mastery is the realm of the chosen few, those born with a special mind, a special spark. However, science and spellwork tell a different story.

In the 1990s, psychologist **K. Anders Ericsson** introduced the idea of *deliberate practice*: not just repetition, but focused, feedback-driven effort designed to push you just beyond your current limits. His research challenged the idea that elite performers in music, chess, and athletics were born exceptional. He argued that *structured learning over time* was a far more powerful force than most people realized.

This became the foundation of countless books, *Peak*, *Grit*, and yes, even the now-famous (and often misunderstood) "10,000-hour rule".

Here's what the science really says:

> Thousands of hours of purposeful practice can make a massive difference. Innate traits may influence the path. But they rarely dictate the destination. Consistent effort often matters more. And curiosity-fueled effort, repeated over time, can change everything.

Later research, like **Macnamara's 2014 meta-analysis**, found that while practice explains a significant portion of skill development. Other factors, like environment, genetics, and opportunity, still matter.

Here's the truth Wizards hold close:

You don't always control your starting point, but you control how often you open the book.

Most of what we call "natural talent" is really just unseen effort. The quiet work done offstage, in silence, with no applause. The kind of learning that happens when no one is watching. The kind that stacks over time, one session at a time, until it becomes magic.

Wizards understand the robe doesn't make the mage, that the ritual does.

So if you've ever said to yourself, *"I'm just not wired for this",* take a moment for yourself. Ask where that voice came from. Whether it's worth listening to, because you don't need to be gifted. You just need to keep going.

Wizards aren't born, they're built. One deliberate spell at a time.

Wizards Among Us

You don't need a staff or a spellbook to live like a Wizard. You just need curiosity, persistence, and a hunger to understand the world more deeply. There are Wizards among us and these people shape their lives through learning.

People who never stop asking "Why?"

Many cite Leonardo da Vinci as the ultimate Renaissance Wizard. He was a painter, an engineer, an anatomist, and a visionary. He didn't become that way because of talent alone. He filled over **7,000 pages** of notes with ideas, sketches, and questions. He imagined flying machines centuries before flight was possible. His notebooks were his spellbooks, and his life was one long quest into the unknown.

Centuries later, another Wizard would step into the cosmos. Not with a telescope alone, but with poetry, perspective, and a mission to help us all feel the wonder of science.

Carl Sagan wasn't just an astronomer. He was a conjurer of curiosity. He made the universe feel personal, accessible, even magical. Through shows like *Cosmos* and books like *Pale Blue Dot*, he reminded us that we are "a way for the cosmos to know itself". He didn't simplify science to make it palatable. He elevated it and made it beautiful. He believed that wonder and logic didn't cancel each other out; they danced.

That's Wizardry, and Wizards aren't just in history books or science specials. Some walk among us, live on our screens, or even stand in the middle of hurricanes.

Jim Cantore, for example — He's not just a meteorologist. He's a storm chaser, a science communicator, a real-life embodiment of elemental magic. He stays where others evacuate, not for thrills, but to *understand*. To observe and to explain the forces most people fear.

What makes Cantore a Wizard isn't the wind-blown camera shots or viral moments. It's the reverence he brings to nature's chaos. The way he *communicates* complexity with clarity and awe. The curiosity that never left him, even after decades of chasing storms.

He once said, *"There's nothing more powerful than understanding what's happening in the sky above us."*

That's Wizard thinking.

He doesn't just forecast the weather. He studies it; translates it. He invites others into the wonder. Wizards aren't defined by the subject they study. Whether it's clouds, code, or constellations. It's the mindset that sets them apart. They don't ask, *"What do I need to know?"* They ask, *"What else is there to discover?"* Then they chase it.

Into libraries
Into labs
Into hurricanes
Into the stars

Apprentice Spell: Your Spell for This Chapter

Think of something you've quietly told yourself you're "just not good at."
Now ask:

- Have I really given it enough time?
- Have I let myself be bad at it without quitting?
- Have I tried learning it in my way, not theirs?

Then do one thing:

Recast the spell.

Try again. Not for mastery or for validation, just to remind yourself that you *can*. You're not lacking talent. You're still casting.

You're still becoming.

The First Spell

The First Spell Isn't Original (And That's Good)

Your first spell doesn't have to be brilliant, original, or even fully yours.

It just has to be cast.

This is where most people freeze. Not because they don't want to grow, but because they believe the first thing they make has to be *great*. That it has to be unique, inspired, or even master-level. Something that proves they belong on the path.

Experienced Wizards, they know better.

No one starts with fireballs and teleportation circles. The first spell is a whisper borrowed from another mage's scroll. Imitation is not a flaw in the system, it *is* the system. Before the spell becomes yours, you copy it. You study the rhythm; you mimic the structure and you cast it as best you can, using someone else's words, cadence, or code. Then something strange happens. It works. Maybe not perfectly or even powerful, but something *clicks.*

That's the first spell.

It's not about creating something new, it's about learning what it takes to create *at all*.

Copy the Spells

I remember the first time I tried running a Dungeons & Dragons campaign. I was beyond excited. I had pages of ideas, half-written lore, custom characters, and branching paths that twisted like a maze. But the closer I got to launch, the more I realized something. I had no idea how to *start*.

I had a thousand ideas, but no opening move. No spell prepared.

So I turned to the scrolls of more experienced Wizards. I read through pre-made campaigns, looking for a spark. I found nothing that felt *perfect*, but I started noticing the way stories flowed. How the exposition worked, even how pacing carried tension. I made notes, lots and lots of them, and despite all of that, I wasn't confident yet.

Then I turned to the show, *Critical Role*. Watching Matt Mercer, how he started games, how he used tone, how he created an atmosphere with just his voice, and it was mesmerizing. I wanted that level of presence, that immersion, that control of the arcane.

So I did what all apprentices do. I studied him.

I started re-watching specific moments, wrote lines that spoke to me, I even practiced his cadence. I noted the way he welcomed players into the world and I planned to open my campaign using a full section of his introduction, almost word-for-word.

And then... something shifted.

A few days before the game, I was testing it aloud, and the words were solid. The pacing was right, but it didn't *feel* like me. Something about it didn't sit right, not because it was wrong, but because it wasn't mine. So I kept the structure, borrowed a line or two, but I rewrote the rest. I blended my language, my rhythm, my tone, with just enough Mercer flavor to keep the magic, but reshaped to fit my voice.

The game started, and it worked. The players became fully engaged. The story? It was *mine*.

That was my first proper spell.

Structure Before Style

We think originality means doing something no one has ever done. But true originality doesn't ignore structure, it builds on it.

Musicians don't start with symphonies. They start with scales.
Painters don't start with masterpieces. They copy sketches from the masters.
Coders don't start with custom apps. They copy snippets from tutorials and GitHub threads.

Every great spellcaster starts by tracing runes they didn't invent. The mistake isn't copying. The mistake is staying stuck there forever. The goal isn't just to imitate, it's understanding. To study the logic behind the lines, to see how the magic works, and then reshape it to serve *your* intention.

Copying teaches form.
Remixing teaches flow.

Then your voice lives somewhere between the two.

When Copying Becomes Craft

There's a moment every learner hits, when the copy no longer feels like a copy. You adjust naturally, deciding without notes. You change elements, not to be different, but because something deeper in you knows what feels *right*.

That's the moment your spellcasting shifts.

I've seen this happen in code. At first, I followed tutorials word-for-word. Then one day, I just stopped. I no longer needed to pause, I just started tweaking things on the fly, rewriting functions before the video told me to. I didn't think, "I'm done copying." I just realized that I wasn't copying anymore.

This happens in writing, too. You imitate a structure, a style or even a voice. Then slowly, your tone creeps in, and your cadence shapes the rhythm. While the bones remain borrowed, the soul is now yours.

Real-World Wizards Do It Too

This isn't just for apprentices, experienced Wizards do this constantly as well.

Stephen King said he mimicked the style of Lovecraft and Bradbury before finding his own voice.
Tarantino famously built his early films by remixing scenes and techniques from movies he loved.
Jimi Hendrix took Bob Dylan's "All Along the Watchtower" and transformed it into something so iconic, *Dylan started performing it Hendrix's way*.

In modern storytelling, **Matt Mercer and Brennan Lee Mulligan**, they blend decades of TTRPG tradition, stage performance, and voice acting into something fresh. Their style didn't just appear from nowhere; it was a culmination, a remix, and now others are learning from him.

Even your heroes had heroes.
Even Archmages copied their first spell.

The Danger of Staying a Copy

Copying is how we start, but it can't be how we stay. There's a moment when the spell stops fitting, when the words feel wrong, when the method limits rather than guides. That's the sign it's time to evolve.

If you're following someone else's template and feel:

- Disconnected from the outcome
- Reliant on instructions instead of intuition
- Afraid to deviate because it might "fail"

Then it's time to break the pattern.

Wizards don't cast forever from someone else's scroll, eventually, they write their own.

The Remix Is the Spell

People don't find originality in isolation, it's found in *remixing* what came before.

Taking a structure you respect.
Breaking it open.
Folding your voice into it.

Then, turning someone else's incantation into your own transformation. That's spellwork, and that's what makes you a Wizard.

Apprentice Spell: Choose someone whose "magic" you admire.

Pick a storyteller, speaker, coder, leader, designer, a builder. Anyone that resonates with you.

Then:

1. Copy one small part of their spell. Structure. Flow. Style. Something concrete.
2. Use it exactly as-is once. Feel it. Watch how it moves.
3. Then remix it. Swap lines. Shift tone. Break a rule.

What worked? What didn't? What felt *yours*?

This isn't about stealing. It's about *learning to cast*. Every Wizard borrows in the beginning.

Eventually, they write the next scroll.

Awakened

You Did the Thing

You didn't just read; you *showed up.* You turned the page, faced the blank and released the myth of "giftedness." You cast your first spell, even if you borrowed it, and that's not a small step.

That's the hardest one.

This chapter isn't about learning something new, it's about **noticing what has already changed**.

You're not where you were, and you're not who you were. You may not even realize that yet, so pause and look back at how this began. You heard the whisper: *There's more than this, and* you said yes.

You opened the book, and you're still here.

From Learning to Living

Robes, staffs, titles, none of these define a Wizard. They're defined by rhythm, by return. That act of coming back to the page, even if you are unsure, tired, it's what separates a dabbler from a practitioner. You are *practicing* now, and the difference between pretending and practicing is everything.

You're Already Becoming

When I think about what makes an experienced Wizard, it's not the amount of knowledge they carry, it's what they do with it.

In most of the jobs I've had, from tech, to service, to teaching, one thing always ended up happening: I learned, I asked questions, and I figured things out. Then, almost without trying, I became the person others came to. A guide, a resource, a kind of mentor.

I didn't seek that role, and I didn't push for it. Knowledge, when you hold on to it long enough, naturally wants to be shared. Wizards aren't just students, they're *translators*. They take what they've studied and help others see it too, and if you keep going?

That's where you're headed.

This Is Your Milestone

You don't need fireworks to mark progress; you need *awareness*. So take a moment here, at the end of your first circle, to recognize this truth.

You started, you stayed, you cast your first spell, and you began writing your own magic.

This moment is proof that you're not waiting to become a Wizard, you already are one.

A Ritual to Mark the Shift

Try one of these before you turn the page:

- **Write One Sentence** - Something you now believe about yourself that you didn't before you started this book.
- **Name This Spell** – Give your "apprentice phase" a title. Something like "The Spell of Showing Up" or "The Courage to Begin."
- **Choose an Artifact** – A sentence you wrote, a quote you copied, a question that won't leave your mind. Make it sacred. That's the first true entry in your spellbook.

A Note From One Wizard to Another

You don't have to memorize everything and you don't need to prove anything. You just need to keep asking questions, build your spellbook, and keep casting.

That's the path.
That's the practice.
That's the way of the Wizard.

You've awakened.

Let's keep going.

II

The Novice

The spark is lit, the circle drawn, and now the pattern begins. The Novice phase is where raw curiosity becomes craft. Where spells are no longer dreams, but deliberate acts. You'll build rituals, manage your mana, and learn to cast with care. This is the work between the wonder, the rhythm, the structure, and the spell prep that turns practice into power. You've chosen the path. Now you walk it with purpose, not perfectly, but consistently.

Real magic lives in repetition.

Preparation is Power

> **"Chaos doesn't care if you're ready. That's why Wizards are."**
> — The Unknown Archmage

The Circle Always Comes First

Before any true spell is cast, a Wizard draws the circle, not for ceremony, and not for show.

The circle is focus.
It's boundary.
It's intent.

It's the moment you stop treating what you're doing like a random task and start treating it like it matters. Preparation is the circle, and it's the mental shift between reacting and responding. Between hoping things go well and creating conditions where they can. Most people don't draw the circle, they rush in, react on instinct. They wing it, hustle or even grind.

The experienced Wizard knows, if you wait until the storm hits to figure it out, you've already lost your first move.

The Storm That Taught Me That

Sometimes preparation isn't always about studying. Sometimes it's the instincts you built without realizing you were building them.

I grew up in what people in the US call tornado alley. Spring meant sirens, alerts, green skies, and air that hung heavy like the world was holding its breath. It was chaotic, unpredictable, and I was *into it.*

While my siblings were off doing other things, I watched The Weather Channel. I studied storm systems like other kids, studied superheroes, and in my world, Jim Cantore *was* a superhero. A storm-chasing, radar-reading, camera-facing wizard of the skies. I wanted to be like him.

I soaked it up.

How storms formed, what warnings to look for, what the radar "hooks" meant. All the colors, the movement, the pressure. Most people saw a weather report, me, I saw a spell scroll. My mom never made me feel weird about it. She would ask me questions, encouraged me, she let me teach her what I was learning. She probably didn't realize it, but she was handing me my first wand. That was my permission to stay curious.

Then one day, everything I'd picked up quietly, all that background knowledge, it came forward. We had a rather nasty line of storms rolling through. There was wind, hail, the skies turned that strange color. If you've lived through it, you know the one. That sickly green, like nature's own warning flare. We didn't have tornado sirens in our city, and there were no official alerts yet, but I had the Weather Channel on and I was watching the radar like it was a live battle strategy. Then I saw it. A sharp curve forming on the screen, a hook echo. That telltale rotation that meant something dangerous was brewing.

Not tomorrow.
Not in theory.
Now.

I turned to my mom and said, *"We need to move."* She didn't question me. We gathered my younger brother, my older sister, and the pets. We packed ourselves into the tiny linen closet in the hallway, the safest space we had. There was no time for debate and then the world tilted. The wind roared, glass shattered somewhere in the house. The pressure shifted in that eerie way it only does when something massive is passing through. For a few terrifying moments, it felt like the world might rip itself apart. The tornado didn't fully touchdown, but it *started*, and it was close. Closer than anyone would ever want. The funnel began forming nearby, and we felt every second of its hunger before it moved past us and dissolved back into rain.

We were okay. Shaken, but okay. Not because we got lucky, because we were *ready.*

All that time I spent being curious and studying storms? I didn't waste that time, and it wasn't useless trivia. It was a quiet, patient preparation. I drew the circle before needing the spell, and when the chaos came, the spell *cast itself.*

What Drawing the Circle Really Means

Preparation isn't about knowing exactly what's coming, it's about *being ready for who you want to be when it arrives.*

That's what drawing the circle does. It doesn't give you control, it gives you clarity, it tells your nervous system: "This moment matters. I know what I'm about to do, and I'm going to show up with intention." You don't need to know the entire script, and you don't need to predict every challenge. You just need to honor the work enough to *make space for it.*

Wizards understand that magic doesn't show up in chaos.

It shows up in rhythm.
In readiness.
In the breath *before* the casting.

Real Wizards, Real Preparation

This isn't fantasy. Preparation shows up in every domain, and the ones who practice it well? Well, they don't leave it to chance. They don't rush the ritual; they understand whether they call it a routine, a checklist, or a pregame mindset, that *the circle comes first*.

Let's name some Wizards you may already know.

Simone Biles, one of the most decorated gymnast of all time, doesn't start her magic on the mat. Her real spells begin in the breath work, the visualization, the headspace. Before she ever flips, she rehearses every movement in her mind down to the landing. That's not superstition, that's neural-level preparation. Her circle is mental, emotional, and physical. When she steps onto the floor, she's already been there a thousand times.

Barack Obama, during his presidency, he stuck to the same suit colors and meal choices. Why? Because decision fatigue is real. His logic was simple: *"I have too many other decisions to make."* His wardrobe was his circle, a way to preserve mana for the spells that actually mattered, like global crises and national policy. Wizards know where their energy leaks, and they seal those gaps before they cast.

Maya Angelou had a ritual for writing. She'd rent a small hotel room with no art, and no distractions. Just a Bible, a bottle of sherry, a legal pad, and her thoughts. She called it "going into the cave." That space, that quiet, was her circle. She knew words didn't flow in chaos, that they need sanctuary, and she made one every time she wrote.

Fred Rogers, aka Mister Rogers, started every day the same way: a prayer, a weight check, a swim, and putting on his iconic cardigan. That wasn't just a costume, it was a transformation. His ritual wasn't for the cameras. It was for him to center, to ground, to show up fully present for the millions of children he spoke to through the screen.

LeBron James spends over a million dollars a year on his physical and mental upkeep. Recovery, nutrition, massage, sleep tracking. He calls it "body maintenance," but it's really *ritual optimization.* He doesn't just train for game day, he prepares *between* games, so his casting capacity stays high across a long season. That's Wizard-level mana management.

Shonda Rhimes, creator of *Grey's Anatomy*, *Scandal*, and *Bridgerton*, doesn't start by writing finished scenes. She builds walls of sticky notes, with color-coded arcs, and character maps. Her writer's room is a literal spell circle filled with reminders, structure, and space for the unknown. She doesn't wait for inspiration to strike. She prepares a world where it can arrive.

Even in the chaos of science and space, **NASA** draws its circle. The launch checklist for every shuttle includes thousands of data points, multiple simulations, and real-time rehearsals. Not because they expect something to go wrong, but because they *refuse to be caught unready if it does.* When the mission launches, the real casting begins, but it only works because the spell was prepped in full.

It's not just the famous icons that do this. Wizards walk beside us, too. I happen work with one of them. Her name is **Alexa,** and she started off in the storm. Working in a fast-paced, often chaotic role as a social media engager for our company. There was no script, no safety net, just a lot of public posts and a constant stream of questions, confusion, and the occasional fire.

She still showed up every day.

She learned the products and learned about our customers. She talked to them like they were long-lost friends, answered questions with warmth and confidence. She made people feel seen, but what truly set her apart was the way she *prepared.* She didn't wing it. She studied past conversations, took notes, looked for patterns, and she built processes inside the chaos. Over time, that preparation added up, and she didn't just get better at her role… she expanded it.

Now, she leads both engagement and customer service. The rituals she used to rely on personally? They've become the blueprint for the entire team, a living document, shared spells, a system that amplifies her work through others.

That's not just management.

That's Wizardry.

What Wizards Do Instead

Wizards don't chase adrenaline. They build rhythm; they prepare spells even when they don't feel inspired, and they write notes. They leave reminders for future-selves or they create systems that carry them when motivation disappears, because motivation *always* disappears.

What you build in stillness carries you into chaos. Preparation is how you keep casting when you're tired, foggy, uncertain. It's not a safety net, it's a ritual of respect.

What It Actually Looks Like

Let's break the spell down.

Preparation doesn't mean grinding your soul into a system. It can be simple, soft, even quiet.

For example, it could be:

- Laying out a journal and pen the night before so your thoughts have a place to land
- Blocking 20 minutes to think before you open an email and let everyone else steer your day
- Creating a tiny phrase or motion, *"We begin now"*, to switch your brain from "scroll" to "spell" mode.
- Writing your key ideas for tomorrow's meeting while you're still fresh, not at the last minute
- Leaving a glass of water by the bed because you know that the tomorrow-you, they deserve to be hydrated without deciding

These are tiny things, but they speak volumes.

They say: *I believe what I'm doing matters, and I care enough to meet it well.*

If You Don't Prepare, You Don't Cast, You React

Let's be real. If you skip the circle, the magic fizzles, or worse, it can backfire.

You don't get flow. You get friction.
You don't get clarity. You get confusion.

Unprepared moments cost mana and they can leave you drained and doubting. They make you feel you're failing, when really, you're just *freestyling without a ritual.*

Wizards don't react.

They respond, because they *prepared* to.

The Wizard's Way Forward

Preparation doesn't shine, it doesn't sparkle, but it *sustains you.*

It's the quiet power behind every confident step, the reason your future self can keep going. You don't need to get it perfect. You just need to show up like it matters, because when the next storm hits, externally or inside your own mind, you won't panic.

You'll reach for the spell you already prepared, and you'll cast it.

Novice Ritual: Draw One Small Circle

Pick something in your life that normally drains you. Something you avoid, dread, or power through on fumes.

Now ask: **How can I draw the circle *before* I step into it?**

Examples:

- If mornings are messy, set out your clothes, notebook, and a glass of water before bed.
- If meetings leave you scattered, write your three key points the night before.
- If creative work feels heavy, start with a warm-up ritual: one playlist, one breath, one sentence.

- If you avoid your goals, write a permission slip: *"I don't need to finish. I just need to begin."*

You don't need a 10-step plan, you just need to draw one small circle.

Then step into it with care.

Ritual Casting

> **"Magic isn't found in the moment. It's built in the rhythm."**
> — The Unknown Archmage

What a Spell Really Looks Like

You've drawn the circle, you've made space, and you're ready to begin.

Now what? Now you cast, not once, not big, not dramatically, but you cast small. You cast often, and you cast again.

This is the part where most people will hesitate. They wait for motivation, for clarity, for the perfect moment, but Wizards know: **magic doesn't arrive fully formed, that it's built in repetition.** Real spells aren't lightning bolts. They're rituals, small, repeatable actions, shaped by intent and powered by rhythm. They don't feel magical at first. They feel ordinary, but with each repetition, they reshape your reality.

Ritual vs. Routine

There's a difference.

A routine is something you do on autopilot.
A ritual is something you do on purpose.
Routine makes the coffee, but a ritual makes the moment mean something.

The behavior might look the same from the outside, but the mindset is different. A ritual adds presence, and it will tell your brain *this matters.*

When I started journaling in the mornings, it wasn't a "routine." It was five minutes of spellwork. One question, one page, one check-in with me. Some days it flowed, while some days it didn't, but it was never about volume. It was about the rhythm. The moment I lit a candle or poured the coffee, my brain knew what was coming. That's ritual casting. It's not what you do. It's how you hold it.

What I Tried That Didn't Work

Not every ritual works. There were times I told myself I was going to work out every morning. I would wake up early, do a quick workout, shower, and then step into the day like I had my life together. I set the alarm, got up, did the thing, for three days in a row. Then came day four. The alarm went off, and I hit snooze.

I was tired, and I didn't feel motivated.

I started negotiating with myself under the covers, and just like that, the "ritual" unraveled. Not because I was lazy, not because I didn't care, but because I was trying to force someone else's idea of what a successful morning looked like.

It wasn't my spell.

I had to realize that a ritual doesn't stick because it's perfect; it sticks because it *fits,* because it *resonates,* because it *gives something back.* A ritual isn't about copying someone else's routine, it's about creating something that holds *you.* That it matches your energy, your life, your rhythm.

The goal isn't to impress anyone. The goal is to cast something that actually works for you.

Wizards in the Wild

You don't have to call it magic for it to be magic. Some of the most focused and intentional people in the world rely on simple, powerful rituals to create structure, unlock flow, and step into who they're becoming.

Haruki Murakami, the acclaimed novelist, runs six miles a day. Every day. When writing a novel, he wakes at 4:00 A.M., writes for five to six hours, then runs, reads, and listens to music. He calls it "a form of mesmerism." A self-induced trance to keep the creative energy moving. The routine isn't strict for discipline's sake. It's how he *stays inside the spell.*

Patrick Rothfuss, author of *The Name of the Wind,* has spoken often about his slow, meticulous writing process. His work isn't about speed, it's about depth, revision after revision, tuning every sentence until it lands just right. He's described storytelling as something closer to shaping than writing, summoning the right words, refining their tone, chasing the rhythm. His process might not be flashy, but it's deliberate, it's focused. A ritual in motion.

Chef Dominique Crenn, the first woman in the U.S. to earn three Michelin stars, begins each day in her kitchen by personally greeting her team, inspecting ingredients, and reviewing every detail. She's not micromanaging, she's connecting. The ritual is her way of aligning energy before creation begins. Her food is art, her kitchen is a sanctum, and her rituals shape both.

David Lynch, filmmaker and visual artist, has meditated twice a day for over 40 years. Rain or shine, production or rest. He treats it like brushing his teeth, non-negotiable. "It's like diving within," he says. "You catch ideas at a deeper level." His ritual isn't flashy, but it's what lets him go deep, stay strange, and keep creating.

Yo-Yo Ma, the world-renowned cellist, still warms up with scales every single day. Not because he needs the practice, but because it brings him into the present. Even after thousands of performances, the ritual keeps him rooted. It says: *This matters.* It says: *I'm here.*

These aren't just routines, they're choices made with care. Circles drawn before action, presence before performance, and they don't wait for inspiration.

They *prepare* for it, and then they cast.

Be Careful: Not Every Ritual is Magical

There's a risk here. Sometimes, we keep doing something not because it's helpful, but because we're afraid to stop. That's not a ritual, but a ritual *without intention.*

Like doomscrolling first thing in the morning. That's a ritual, not a good one, but still a spell you're casting.

Complaining before you've tried, doubting yourself before you begin, always saying yes before checking your energy. These are unspoken rituals too and they shape us just as much as the conscious ones.

The question you have to ask yourself is: **Do your rituals make you feel**

more like a Wizard or less?

Naming Your Spells

Naming a ritual gives it power. When you name something, your brain recognizes it as meaningful. It stops being background noise and becomes a choice.

Try this:

- Morning coffee becomes **"the Spell of Stillness"**
- A quick stretch after lunch becomes **"the Mana Reset"**
- Sending your daily priorities to your team becomes **"the Focus Beacon"**
- Reading one page before bed becomes **"the Final Incantation"**

This isn't just fun, it's functional. Names create memory. They make your life feel like a story you're actively shaping, not just surviving, and that's the goal here.

You're not just going through the day, you're casting it.

The Wizard's Way Forward

Spells don't cast themselves, magic doesn't move without movement, but you don't need to do it all at once. You just need rhythm.

Repetition.
Intention.

Start with one ritual, something small, and then show up for it.

Again.
And again.

And again.

Because magic isn't found in the moment. It's built in the rhythm.

Novice Ritual: Choose Your First Spellcasting Ritual

Pick one small thing you do (or want to do) every day. Something that could anchor you, steady you, set the tone. Then turn it into a ritual.

Ask:

- What would make this feel intentional?
- How could I begin or end it with a moment of presence?
- What could I name it, so it carries weight?

Examples:

- Before your first task of the day, take one deep breath, light a candle, or write one line. Call it your **Initiation Spell**.
- After work, go for a walk and mentally list three things that restored you today. Call it **Closing the Circle**.
- Before bed, write one sentence: *"Today I cast..."* and finish the thought. That's your **spellbook entry**.

You don't need to overhaul your life, you just need *one* deliberate ritual.

Do it.
Name it.
Keep casting.

56

Mana Management

"**You are not infinite. But you are renewable. **"
— The Unknown Archmage

The Novice's First Lesson

Even wizards need rest. Knowing your limits isn't weakness, it's wisdom.

Wizards don't sprint. They cast, they rest, they recover, then they cast again. Yet in the real world, we treat exhaustion like a badge of honor. We romanticize burnout; we reward the ones who work through lunch, skip vacations, and answer emails at midnight. Ask yourself this: when were you last truly at your best when completely depleted?

The truth is, even in the stories, even in the grandest myths, **all magic has a cost**.

The most powerful Wizards in every tale have limits. They know that power isn't infinite, and that there's a price for every spell. The overextending of your energy, your focus, your will, leads not to greatness, but to collapse. Yet here we are, trying to be heroes without pause, casting spells with no regard for recovery.

But here's the lesson every Wizard learns eventually: **you can't grow if you never rest**. You can't learn if you're always reacting, and you can't cast powerful spells if you never replenish what fuels them.

The Culture of "Always On"

We live in a world that measures worth by output. Hustle culture, toxic productivity, that grind now, rest later mentality. Wizards know better. They know that rest isn't a delay, it's part of the ritual.

If you study elite performers, musicians, athletes, and scientists, you'll find that **recovery is not optional**. It's built into the schedule, and deep rest will balance deep work. The brain needs downtime to process, to connect ideas, to integrate what you've learned. This isn't laziness, it's neuroscience.

Even sleep itself is a form of spell preparation. During REM sleep, your brain consolidates memory and strengthens neural pathways. It doesn't just store what you've learned; it upgrades how you think.

So if you're skipping rest in the name of ambition, you're actually sabotaging your own spellbook.

Real Wizards Know When to Step Back

One of the hardest lessons I had to learn was when *not* to push. For years, I wore burnout like armor. I said yes to every project, stayed up late finishing projects, woke up early to squeeze in more productivity. I thought it strengthened me, made me more dedicated, but in reality, it made me fragmented. I was irritable, and shaky with self-doubt.

My spells were sloppy.
My focus was scattered.
My work suffered and so did my relationships.

It wasn't until I finally stopped, truly stopped, that I realized something. **Clarity lives in the quiet.**

Some of my best insights have come not while grinding, but while walking, driving, journaling, or even just resting. Not because I was trying harder, but because I gave my mind enough space to breathe.

You don't need to earn rest; you need to *honor* it.

Rewriting the Script

We've been told that stepping back is weakness, and that saying no means we're falling behind. Experienced Wizards rewrite the script. We know that **sustainable magic is better than explosive burnout**. That the most powerful thing we can do sometimes is… pause.

So build your rituals of rest.
Step away from the screen.
Say no when your energy is low.

Let silence be your sanctuary. Let the page stay blank for a day if you need it to.

That's not quitting, that's spell prep.

The Limits of Power

Burnout isn't noble, it's neglect. There's a seductive danger in over achievement. It will whisper things like:

Just a little more.
Push through.
You're built for this.

You're not tired, you're just weak.

We hear it from motivational speakers, from bosses, from well-meaning mentors, and after a while, it becomes internalized. We start to believe that *real* success means never stopping. That the ones who win are the ones who *outlast* the rest. Wizards know something the rest of the world forgets:

Power has limits. And when you pretend it doesn't, you break.

The Illusion of "Just One More Spell"

In every campaign, in every book, there's a moment when the Wizard tries to cast one spell too many. They know they're low on energy; they feel the edge fraying, but the pressure is high, the stakes are real, and they whisper to themselves, *Just one more spell.*

In the stories, that moment might lead to a heroic triumph or to collapse. In real life, it usually leads to burnout. I've had those days, weeks, even where I ignored the signs. I would have headaches, brain fog, short temper, poor sleep. My code was buggy and my mind was a jumble. I wasn't creating; I was surviving. I kept going, because I thought that was what being committed looked like.

Turns out, it wasn't.

It was me neglecting my boundaries, mistaking output for worth, pretending I was immune to the laws of energy.

The Wizard's Boundaries

One of the most powerful things a Wizard can do is draw a circle. Not to trap others out, but to protect what's within. Boundaries aren't selfish, they're sacred. Wizards don't throw fire into the dark without intention. They prepare, they rest, they cast *strategically*, not impulsively. They don't spend energy where it won't matter, and when they're low on energy, they don't double down. They withdraw, recharge, and return stronger.

So ask yourself:

- Are you casting spells from overflow or from depletion?
- Are you saying yes to everything out of fear or out of alignment?
- Are you confusing self-sacrifice with contribution?

You are not infinite. But you *are* renewable.

When You Respect the Limits, You Expand Them

Here's the twist. When you *honor* your limits, they shift. Your mind becomes clearer, your work becomes sharper. You recover faster, you learn faster, and you gain resilience. Not by pushing harder, but by resting better. You become more powerful by knowing when to stop.

Rest is not the opposite of growth. It's what allows growth to happen.

This is the lesson too many of us learn late. We think we can shortcut our way to mastery. In reality, **mastery requires margin,** space between the spells and silence between the notes.

Magic doesn't flow through clenched fists. It flows through open hands, steady breath, and a mind that knows when to listen.

The Advice Every Wizard Needs

Not everyone wears the robe, and not everyone will call themselves a Wizard, but everyone knows what it's like to be tired. Deeply tired. The kind that doesn't just sit in your muscles, it settles behind your eyes, in your chest, in the part of you that used to feel excited to learn.

There's a moment, for every one of us, where we hit the wall. Not because we don't care, but because we cared too much for too long without pause.

Here is what I want you to remember.

You are not lazy for needing rest.
Needing time doesn't mean you're broken.
You are not falling behind.
You're just human, and even the wisest Wizards are still that.

Mr. Rogers, once said:

> "I like you just the way you are."

He didn't mean "when you're achieving" or "when you're useful." He meant you in stillness, in softness, in recovery. Rest doesn't make you less of a hero. It's what allows you to rise again.

So take the nap.
Take the walk.
Take the moment to breathe.
Let the scroll stay unrolled for a night.
Let the spellbook close.

The magic isn't going anywhere and when you return, clearer, calmer, renewed. You'll remember why you started this journey in the first place.

Because true Wizards don't burn out. They burn bright and then rest, so they can burn again.

Your Focus is Your Wand

> **"The greatest spells are broken not by force, but by fractured attention."**
> — The Unknown Archmage

The Wand in Your Hand

Every Wizard needs a wand. Not because it holds power, but because it *channels* it. The wand isn't what makes the spell happen, it's what directs it, focuses it. Without a wand, the energy goes everywhere, uncontrolled, unshaped, and unseen.

Your wand? That is your focus.

Where your attention goes, your energy flows. Your will follows, and your our magic takes shape. In the real world, that wand gets yanked from your grip dozens of times a day. Notifications, messages, mental to-do lists, dopamine loops, distractions dressed as urgency. It's no wonder our spells fall apart before they even land.

Most people don't lose power, they just lose *focus,* and when the spell breaks, they blame themselves, not the static.

The Fracture

Every Wizard, at some point, faces it: the fracture. Not of will, not of skill, but of attention. You're in the middle of something important, you're locked in, everything is working.

Then…

Ding.

"Hey, can I grab you for a second?" Another tab, another text, another mental switch. Now you're not casting anymore. You're reacting, you're spinning, you're fragmented.

The spell fizzles, and the worst part is you don't even notice until the smoke clears.

The Cost of Multitasking

We all hear it: *"If you can multitask, you can succeed."*

I've learned the truth: multitasking isn't mastery. It's masked chaos. Sure, sometimes you can juggle, especially in life's daily chaos. That's right, parents, I see you.

Most of the time, it backfires.

There are days at work where I'm dialed in, locked onto a report, cleaning data, solving something complex. Then someone drops a request. I say yes, stop what I am doing and then there is the next ping, just one more favor. Next thing I know, I'm running four tabs in my head, juggling five tasks, and nothing's really landing.

If you've ever worked with data, you know this; focus is your best friend. One stray thought, just one, and suddenly the report's wrong. There is a filter applied to the wrong field, a sort that shifts a whole column and sometimes the worst of all? You might not even notice until the *very end.* Now you're backtracking, trying to find where it broke.

If you've ever coded, this is painfully familiar. You spend hours writing something elegant, you run it, and boom, error. You go line by line, only to realize it was a semicolon, a comma, a missed quote mark. That's the cost of distraction, and when the spell breaks, it can take hours to repair.

Multitasking might feel like progress, but focus, that's where the magic really lives.

Your Focus Is a Channel

When you learn to guard your focus, something shifts. You get more done in less time. You make fewer mistakes, but more importantly, your work *feels* better. You lose the mental whiplash; you enter the flow, and you find a deeper rhythm. This is why Wizards train not just their skills, but their *attention.*

Focus isn't just a productivity tool. It's the wand in your hand, and the sharper you aim it, the stronger your spells become.

The Spellbreakers

Let's name the things that break your focus.

- **Notifications** — every ping is a mana leak.
- **Context switching** — jumping between tasks costs more energy than you think.
- **Open loops** — half-done thoughts, to-do lists, tabs you forgot to close.

- **Noise** — literal or mental. Background chaos scrambles spellcasting.
- **Internal guilt** — the voice saying you should be doing something else.

These are your enemies. They don't feel aggressive, they will feel normal, and that's what makes them dangerous.

So Wizards build shields.

Building a Focus Ritual

The best way to protect your focus? Make it a ritual. Before you begin a task that matters, draw the circle, channel your wand, and prepare your mind.

Try this:

- **Clear your space.** Close tabs. Put your phone away. Clean the desk if you need to.
- **Set a timer.** 25, 45, or 90 minutes. However long you can truly commit.
- **Begin with intention.** One breath. One phrase. *"This matters."*
- **When it ends, step away.** Close the spell. Don't squeeze in another cast.

You don't need all-day discipline. You need short, sacred bursts of undistracted energy.

That's where the power lives.

The Myth of "Always On"

Focus isn't about grinding all day. It's about working with care when it counts. There's a myth that success comes from being "always on", but Wizards know the mind is like a lens. If it's pointed everywhere, it sees nothing clearly. If it's overused, and it cracks.

Focus is a limited resource.
That's why it's sacred.

Don't waste it on things that don't matter. Don't give it away without permission, and whatever you do, don't multitask your magic.

The Wizard's Way Forward

Your magic doesn't just come from what you know. It comes from what you *choose to give your attention to.*

Energy follows attention. Spells follow intention.

So guard it.
Guide it.
Practice it.

You don't need to be perfect, you just need to point your wand with care.

Novice Ritual: The Wand of Attention

Pick one moment today, just one that deserves your full attention. A task, a conversation, a practice, a page. Before you begin, take a breath and set the intention.

"This is the spell I'm casting now."

Then give it your full focus.

No toggling.
No background tabs.
No divided will.
Just presence and power. Just one wand, aimed well.

Afterward, reflect:

- How did it feel?
- What did you notice?
- What changed?

This is how you train.
This is how you cast.
This is how you sharpen the wand you already hold.

Spells Take Time

"Wizards don't chase fast. They cast until the spell remembers its purpose."
— The Unknown Archmage

The Impatience Trap

We're trained to expect instant results, like fast shipping, fast food, and fast feedback. If something doesn't click in a day, we assume we did it wrong. If we're not amazing at it by week two, we call ourselves untalented. If it doesn't grow fast, it must be dying.

Wizards know real magic doesn't explode into existence. It builds, layer by layer, and cast by cast. Sometimes, nothing happens at first. Sometimes, even after effort and care, the spell doesn't land. Not yet.

That doesn't mean it's not working, it just takes time. This is where the novice often struggles. They expect spells to work on the first try, but spells aren't wishes.

They're actions. They are choices made with intention, repeated. You cast, you refine, you learn, and you cast again.

That's the rhythm.

What I Learned the Hard Way

A few years ago, I had COVID and was stuck in my room recovering. Anyone who's had it knows, it's not just rough physically, but it's *boring*. I couldn't leave my space, couldn't do much, but at least I had my PlayStation with me.

I've always loved video games, ever since I was a kid. Games like Link, Mario, and Tetris. I grew up with a controller in my hand. So while I was recovering, I started playing **Baldur's Gate 3**. The game had just come out, and I was texting with my brother, telling him how fun it was. He said, "You should stream this so I can watch."

I had never streamed before, so I figured, why not?

I started streaming to Twitch. I didn't use a camera, it was just gameplay and my mic. My brother tuned in every time, chatting with me while I explained mechanics, character builds, and story choices.

Then someone else showed up. Then another.

Apparently, people enjoyed watching me play. Maybe it was the voice, maybe it was the vibe, but whatever it was… something was clicking. After I recovered, I decided to stick with it. I got a camera, built a layout, then I started streaming a few times a week.

Within a month, I was averaging 15+ viewers per stream. Then just a short few months later, I became a **Twitch Affiliate**. I was building something, and I was getting better. I was having *fun,* and then life did what it does best.

My older cat, Loki, got sick, and I started skipping streams. One here, one there. My time became vet visits, quiet nights with him curled up by me. I had a feeling he wouldn't be around much longer, and I wanted to be present.

Then… it stopped.

The streams I had been casting,that momentum, that spell. It just fizzled away.

Two years went by. I never came back to it, and the truth? I still think about it, but not with guilt, with *awareness*. I was building something real. I was in the middle of a spell, but I didn't finish casting it. Sometimes life shifts, sometimes we pause for the right reasons, but sometimes… we stop too soon. When that happens, we don't just lose the moment; we lose what might've come next.

Most Spells Don't Work Immediately

That's not failure. That's *reality*.

Progress is weird. It's slow, uneven, quiet. You show up, put in the work, and feel like nothing's happening, and then suddenly, it lands. The only way it gets there is if you keep casting.

Think about the way trees grow. The roots deepen before anything breaks the surface.

Think about how long a melody takes to master. How long it takes to build trust. What about getting good at a game, writing a book, recovering, or to just grow.

Spells take time.

If you give up too early, you never see what they could've become.

Not Working ≠ Not Working

You aren't wasting your effort just because you can't see results yet. A spell cast today might not bloom until next month. That routine you're practicing might feel small now, but it's laying the foundation. That habit you're building might not show external results, but it's already shifting who you are.

Wizards don't demand fast.

They stay in the work.

They trust the rhythm, and they cast until it lands.

Culture Moves Fast. Magic Doesn't Have To.

We live in a world obsessed with speed. Viral videos, overnight success. Things like "How I gained 100,000 followers in 3 days."

But that's not how real growth works. Not creatively, not spiritually, not sustainably. If you only chase speed, you'll start rushing spells, you'll cast sloppily, you'll skip the steps that give your work soul. You'll burn out or give up because the result didn't arrive on time.

Wizards play the long game. They don't rush the magic.

The Wizard's Way Forward

Some of your best work won't show results right away. Some of your strongest spells will unfold slowly, quietly, imperfectly.

And some things you almost gave up on, they might've been your break-through, if you'd just stayed with them a little longer.

Wizards don't chase fast.

And when the spell finally lands? They've already begun the next.

They trust the process.
They stay steady.
They cast until it works.

Novice Ritual: The Long Spell

Pick something you're working on right now.

Something slow, maybe something that *hasn't landed yet*. It could be a creative project, a habit, a skill, or a healing process. Something that matters to you, but feels like it's going nowhere.

Now write this phrase:
   "This spell takes time. I'm still casting it."

Put it somewhere you'll see it, and the next time you feel like quitting or wondering why it's not working fast enough, remember: you're not failing.

You're just in the middle of the spell.

Keep casting.

Arise

> **"You no longer wait for the spell to work. You have become the reason it does."**
> — The Unknown Archmage

You've drawn the circle, and you cast your first spells. You've built rituals, protected your energy, and practiced showing up, not perfectly, but with intention. You've started becoming a Wizard, not because someone handed you a wand, but because you stopped waiting to feel ready... and started creating your own rhythm.

The Novice's Journey

You've done what most never even try. You're no longer just reacting, you prepare. You don't wait on motivation; you are protecting your mana. Instead of juggling chaos, you now focus with intention. You've let go of the pull of overnight results, and started casting long spells... trusting that's enough.

You may not feel like an expert yet, and that is good.

This stage wasn't about mastery. It was about movement; it was about building the inner architecture to hold deeper magic.

What I Had to Learn

There was a time when I believed I needed to *feel confident* before I could act. Like confidence was the spell, and action was the result. That wasn't true.

Action was the spell, and confidence, well it came later.

Taking that first step, even when I didn't feel ready, that's what changed things. That's what gave me evidence I could keep going.

Another thing, learning to say no, not out of avoidance, but out of alignment. That's when the real shift happened. When I stopped spending my energy trying to prove I could do everything and started spending it where it actually mattered.

That's when I stopped just knowing the spells and started casting like they belonged to me.

You've Earned This

If you've read this far, done the rituals, reflected, even just paused long enough to *consider* a different way of moving through the world, you've already changed.

You've started thinking like a Wizard.

I know... using this stuff in the real world? It's not always easy, life still gets messy, old habits will still pull hard, but chaos doesn't stop just because you're learning.

You've got something now.

Process.

Language.
Rhythm.

A way to know when the magic is missing and how to bring it back. Be proud of what you've built. You've started shaping your life on purpose and soon, you'll be seeing magic everywhere because you'll have the clarity to notice it.

Soon, you'll be an Archmage of your own.

What Comes Next

In the next part of this journey, we go deeper.

You've learned how to cast and now you'll learn *what kind of Wizard you are.*

In *The Initiate*, the spells get personal.

We'll talk about identity, self-trust, and learning how to learn. We will break old curses, finding wisdom beneath information and it won't be just about what you do. It's about who you become while doing it.

For now?

Pause.
Breathe.
Acknowledge this chapter.

You don't rise because you're perfect. You rise because the work is worth it.
You don't rise because the spell is done. You rise because it's *yours* now.
You don't rise because you're ready. You rise because you've already begun.

You're further than you think.

III

The Initiate

You've come farther than most. Where others only dip a toe into the stream of magic, you've begun to wade in. You've studied, you've questioned, you've felt the stirring of something ancient in your bones.

But now comes the turning point.

The Initiate stage isn't about collecting knowledge, it's about becoming changed by it.

The Library is Infinite

> **"Every question is a doorway. The Library opens to the ones who keep walking."**
> — The Unknown Archmage

The Library Without Walls

A Wizard's journey doesn't begin with answers. It begins with *questions*, and questions live in libraries.

Not just the kind with neat rows of books and whispering rules. No, I'm talking about the Library Without Walls, the infinite one, the strange one, the one that only reveals itself when you're ready to step off the path and into wonder.

You've been there before, whether or not you knew it. It's the rabbit hole you fell into after asking, *"Wait, how do they make glass?"* The video you watched at 2AM that explained why time feels faster as we age, or at that moment you looked up from your phone and thought, *I wonder who first figured this out.*

The Library Without Walls doesn't have hours, it never closes. It lives in podcasts, notebooks, and Google searches that spiral into something beautiful. It hides in conversations with brilliant strangers. It shines through in documentaries, late-night thoughts, and childhood questions that remain unanswered. The deeper you go, the more it gives you back.

Most people forget this library exists. They get older, busier, tired. They trade curiosity for certainty, and before long, their world shrinks to routines and to-do lists.

Safe.
Efficient.
Predictable.

But empty.

Not for Wizards. We know that *not knowing* isn't a threat, that it's an invitation. Every gap in understanding is a portal, every question is a key, and every moment we ask "Why?" or "What else?" we're opening a new wing of the library. One built by us, for us.

I've spent years collecting scrolls, notes in Notion, half-read books, quotes scribbled in notebooks, questions I've never fully answered. Not because I'm chasing mastery, but because I *enjoy getting* lost in the stacks. I like the feeling of a sentence re-wiring my brain. I enjoy wondering how something works, and then following that thread until it changes how I see the world.

That's what being a Wizard is. Not knowing everything, but *never giving up on learning anything.*

So here's your reminder.
You don't need permission to explore.
You don't need credentials to be curious.
The Library Without Walls is already around you and it's been waiting, just like you.

This isn't the first time you've been here, but this may be the first time you've noticed.

The Power of Self-Taught Growth

You don't need a classroom to learn. You just need the right question.

When I was younger, the internet was just starting to creep into everyday life. It wasn't fast, nor was it sleek. It screeched every time it connected, like some arcane ritual that demanded a sacrifice before it would reveal the mysteries of the universe, but once that static faded and the connection was established?

The world opened up.

Suddenly, I had something I never realized I'd been missing: access. Access to knowledge, to answers, to questions I didn't even know how to ask yet. One thing that had always fascinated me was space. Even before I knew the names of constellations, I'd stare up at the stars and feel that pull, the sense that there was something out there. Something worth reaching for.

I wanted to go to space camp. I wanted to explore the stars, to see the blackness between the lights and understand what made it sing. I never made it to space camp, but I found something else. I found a path, a portal, a rabbit hole with no bottom.

One night, I was watching a documentary on black holes, how they bend time, how their gravity shapes everything around them. The documentary ended, but I still had questions. I needed to know even more, so I sat at the computer, dialed in, and started searching.

Stars.
Nebulas.

Quasars.
Wormholes.

One question led to another, and each answer opened a new door. I didn't understand all of it, not at first, but I didn't care. It wasn't about mastery, and knowing everything right away, it was about discovery. I wanted to *see the shape of the unknown*. That one documentary didn't give me a full education, but it gave me a direction, and that direction taught me something deeper than any textbook ever could:

Having access to answers is great, but learning how to ask better questions?

Now that's the real magic.

I didn't know it yet, but perhaps that's when I started to really understand what it meant to think like a Wizard. To not wait for someone to assign the lesson, to not hope that someone would explain it to me, but to chase the wonder. To follow the thread, to treat curiosity not as a distraction, but as a compass.

I never became an astronaut, but that night, sitting at a humming computer in the dark, lit only by a screen and a sense of wonder?

That moment didn't change where I was, but it changed who I was becoming.

Wandering with Intention

Some spells don't look like effort. They look like drifting, like daydreaming, or like staring out the window at nothing in particular and feeling something stir. Wizards know it's not a distraction, but the work beneath the work.

Every time you follow a question no one asked you to answer, you build something unseen. You widen your mental map, deepen your capacity for wonder, step off the road you were told to follow, and you discover a path only you could walk. It doesn't always lead somewhere useful, and that's not the point.

Sometimes you chase an idea only to abandon it halfway.
Sometimes you fill pages with notes that no one will read.
Sometimes you ask a question that leaves you with more questions.
It might feel like wandering, but it's not wasted. The Library remembers every step, every half-thought scribbled in a notebook, every tab you forgot to close. It will remember every late-night video that changed how you see time, or memory, or mushrooms, or gravity.

That's all part of the spell.

You may not know what it's for yet, but the magic is storing itself, and one day, you'll need something and it'll be there. A metaphor that reshapes a conversation, a strange fact that helps you solve a real problem, or maybe a line you underlined years ago that suddenly feels like a key.

That's how Wizards grow. Not in a straight line, not always with proof, but in spirals, in sparks, in curiosity that leaves a trail behind them.

So go deeper.
Get lost.
Read something strange.
Reread something sacred.

Let it rewire you, because real learning doesn't always feel productive, it feels alive. It feels like remembering something you never knew, and when the time comes to use what you've found, you won't have to dig.

It'll already be a part of you.

Rituals for the Lifelong Learner

Wizards don't wait for permission to grow. They make learning a ritual, a habit, a daily act of curiosity and commitment, because real growth doesn't come from a single breakthrough. It comes from small, consistent moments where you choose to stay curious.

These rituals aren't grand. They're not flashy, but they're powerful, because they remind you that learning is something you *do*, not just something you *believe in*.

Here are a few simple practices to build your own Wizard's ritual.

Read One Scroll a Week

Pick a book, article, blog post, or research paper that challenges you, even just a little. Don't just scroll; study, annotate, ask, "What does this teach me about the world… and about myself?"

This isn't about speed, it's about depth. One scroll can hold more wisdom than a thousand tweets.

Journal Your Questions Before You Google Them

In the age of instant answers, we've lost something sacred: *the question itself.*

Instead of rushing to look things up, write the question down first. Sit with it, think about what you *hope* the answer is. What it *might* be, or why it matters to you. Then search, but bring your thoughts with you.

Sometimes the path to the answer teaches you more than the answer itself.

Keep a Wonder List

Make space for questions that don't have deadlines.

- Why do we dream?
- Could plants communicate in ways we haven't measured yet?
- What would happen if we all read more poetry than news?

These aren't tasks, they're invitations. Keep them in a note, a journal, a digital scroll. Revisit them, add to them, let them remind you that life isn't about knowing everything.

It's about staying open.

Build a Spellbook

Start gathering your own magic.

Not spells in the fantasy sense, but tools, techniques, and truths that feel like power when you read them. A line from a book, framework from a podcast, or a principle that changed the way you see things. Give each one a title, a purpose, a context.

Your spellbook can be a Notion page, a Moleskine, a folder on your desktop. What it is doesn't matter. What matters is that it grows with you.

Start a Study Ritual

Pick one time each week to study something that has *nothing* to do with your job or your goals.

Just study for the joy of it. Learn something wildly unrelated. Want to understand how bridges work? Cool. Want to figure out how bees navigate?

Excellent. Want to watch a documentary on ancient ink-making? Yes, Wizard. Do that.

Every time you learn without a purpose, you expand your spellcasting range.

The Ritual of Curiosity

You don't become a Wizard by collecting degrees, titles, or accolades. You become one by listening to the quiet pull of wonder and choosing to follow it. Not once, or when it's convenient, but again and again, as a ritual.

So read the scrolls, chase the stars, study the storms. Not to be impressive, but to stay awake, because the world will try to lull you into certainty. It will hand you answers before you've learned how to ask. We Wizards, we will remember, every question is a doorway and every act of curiosity is a spell.

The Library Without Walls is still open.
It always has been. It always will be.
And your next spell is already waiting. All that's left to do…

is cast it.

Intelligence vs Wisdom

> **"Intelligence builds the spell. Wisdom knows when not to cast it."**
> —The Unknown Archmage

The Difference Most Miss

There's a subtle shift that happens in every Wizard's journey. So subtle, in fact, that many miss it. It's the moment you realize you're not here just to learn spells.

You're here to decide when to use them.

At first, intelligence feels like everything. You're consuming knowledge, gathering insight, memorizing systems. You're making connections. You feel sharper, more equipped, more powerful than you've felt in years, maybe ever.

That's not wrong, but the real growth starts when you realize intelligence is only part of the magic. That it teaches you what you can do.

Wisdom teaches you what you should do.

That's what this chapter is about. Knowing the difference and choosing the harder path.

A Moment You Might Recognize

You've probably seen something like this before.

There's someone in the room who clearly knows their stuff. Maybe it's at work, in a class, or during a group project. They've read the manuals, memorized the process, and probably have a spreadsheet for every situation. When a problem pops up, they're quick to jump in with the fix, clear, confident, and correct.

And yet… something about the way they handle it makes things worse.

Maybe it's how they correct someone in front of others.
Maybe it's the tone, just sharp enough to sting.
Maybe it's that they're so focused on being right, they forget there's a human being on the other side of the mistake.

They don't mean harm, but their intelligence is untempered. It shows up as urgency, control, precision without pause, and the result? Trust erodes, people retreat, and the "fix" ends up costing more than the original problem.

That's the moment you see the difference:

Intelligence solves the issue.
Wisdom considers the impact.

Intelligence Is the Spellbook

Let's be clear, intelligence matters. It's what gives you options, spells, and tools. Specifically, the ability to analyze, understand, and act.

It's essential to becoming a Wizard, but it can also become a trap.

Intelligence can become performative, more display than depth.
It can serve your ego more than your growth.
It can make you think being right is the same thing as being effective.
It's not.

Intelligence is a sharp wand, but without wisdom, it cuts the wrong things.

Wisdom Is the Spellcaster

Wisdom isn't louder, it's quieter. It doesn't interrupt; it listens longer, and it makes space.

Where intelligence rushes in, wisdom holds back.

Wisdom asks:

- Is now the right time?
- Is this the right place?
- Will this help or just prove I know something?

Wisdom is the part of you that slows down before sending that email. It's the breath you take before responding. It's the choice to listen instead of lecture, even when you know you're right.

That's not weakness. That's mastery.

How to Know Which One You're Using

Here's a simple check-in:

When you speak, solve, or act. Ask yourself:

- Am I trying to help, or trying to prove?
- Am I listening, or waiting for my turn to talk?
- Am I showing up as the person I want to be or just the smartest person in the room?

These questions won't always give you comfortable answers, but they'll give you true ones.

That's wisdom talking.

You Learn Wisdom by Living

Wisdom doesn't show up after reading a book, it shows up after living one.

You gain it by making the wrong call and owning it. By realizing the fix made things worse. By noticing the tension you caused and doing better next time.

It's slow magic, but it's realm and once you start practicing it, people will feel the difference around you, without knowing why.

Rituals for Cultivating Wisdom

Want to start building it on purpose?

Try this:

1. Pause Before You Speak

Especially when emotions are high. Breathe. Count to three. See what shifts.

2. Practice Reflective Listening
Repeat back what someone says before responding. This isn't about parroting. it's about showing that you heard them, fully.

3. Journal Your Interactions
At the end of the day, ask: Where did I respond wisely? Where did I default to being right?

Write honestly. No one else will see it.

4. Seek Out the Quiet Mentors
Wisdom often hides in people who aren't loud about it. The coworker who doesn't interrupt, the friend who lets silence breathe. Take a moment and watch them.

The Balance You're Building

The goal isn't to stop being smart. The goal is to pair your sharpness with softness, your mind with your presence.

To become the kind of Wizard who doesn't just know a thousand spells… But understands which one to use, and when.

You're not here to win every argument. You're here to weave impact with intention.

That right there? That takes more than a spellbook.

That takes you.

Your Wisdom Quest

Tonight, find a quiet place. Sit with this question:

"Where in my life am I trying to be right... more than I'm trying to be wise?"

Write your answer.

It doesn't need to be long, just honest. Then, choose one moment tomorrow to practice restraint.

Pause.
Listen.
Ask instead of answer.
That's the spell.

Scrolls, Tomes, and Trials

What the Scrolls Teach You

Every Wizard begins with the scrolls. They are quick lessons, short truths, highlighted quotes or books that promise "Ten Ways to Change Your Life" and "The Secret to Success in a Single Sentence."

Honestly? They can help.

Scrolls give you language you didn't have. They spark curiosity; they plant seeds, and for many of us, they're the gateway to something deeper.

Here's the catch. The scrolls are only for starting the journey.

They're portable, convenient, fast, designed to be consumed, not wrestled with. You read them once and feel you've learned something. Maybe you have. But scrolls are surface spells. They show you the outlines of magic, not its depth.

And if you're not careful, you'll start mistaking collection for transformation.

You'll stack quotes instead of applying them.
You'll underline paragraphs instead of sitting in silence.
You'll read about vulnerability and still avoid the conversation.

Scrolls are easy to carry. That's what makes them feel safe.

But if you want to level up, you'll need to reach for something heavier.

The Weight of Tomes

Tomes are different. They don't give you straightforward answers. They challenge your assumptions; they take time. You don't just read a tome. You sit with it, re-read it, put it down because it's too much, then pick it back up weeks later and realize you missed half of it the first time.

A tome is the book you didn't finish because it hit too close. It's the chapter you had to read twice, not because you didn't understand it, but because you did. Tomes are slow-burning spells. The kind that doesn't impress you at first glance… but change your direction without you even realizing.

In real life, a tome can be a book, a conversation, or a hard truth someone tells you at exactly the wrong or right time. It's the mentor who doesn't give you advice, but asks you a question that lingers for days. It's the moment you realize your favorite quote doesn't apply to this situation at all. It's the insight that comes not from learning something new, but from seeing something old differently.

Tomes don't give you answers. They give you depth, and depth takes time.

The Trial Is the Real Teacher

You can study all you want. You can memorize scrolls, you can highlight entire tomes, but none of it means anything until you're tested. Not with an exam, but with life.

The trial is when you're tired, frustrated, and everything you learned suddenly feels far away. It's when your confidence breaks, when your routine gets interrupted, or when someone you care about misunderstands you, and no self-help mantra is going to fix it.

It's when your values get tested in public, not just on paper.
When you have to decide if you'll speak up... or stay silent.
When you feel imposter syndrome whispering in your ear, and you have to show up, anyway.

This is where most people stop. They go back to the scrolls, and they think they need to "learn more," but Initiates, they learn the truth. The trial is the classroom.

It's not about what you know, it's about who you are in the moment you're asked to act

Real-Life Magic

Think of the people you truly admire. Not the ones with the most degrees, or the biggest vocabularies.

The ones who walk into a room and bring calm.
The ones who can sit with discomfort without fixing it.
The ones who don't raise their voice to be heard, but everyone listens to when they speak.

You might think of someone like Neil deGrasse Tyson. An astrophysicist, yes, but more than that, he is a communicator. He doesn't just know the universe; he helps others feel it, he brings wonder down to earth. He's intelligent, but what makes him magnetic is how he shares that intelligence, with warmth, clarity, and a sense of play.

Maybe it's someone in your life.

A teacher who made you feel seen, or the coworker who holds space when others rush. A quiet presence who never needed the spotlight, but always held the room.

These people aren't just smart, they're anchored.

They've read the scrolls, they've sat with the tomes, but they've also faced the trial, and it shows.

They didn't just learn magic. They became it.

Scrolls Are for Starting

Tomes Are for Deepening.
Trials Are for Becoming.
This is the journey of every Wizard.

You start wide, scrolls and quotes and fresh ideas. That's good. Then you go deep, books that challenge you, mentors who don't coddle you, mirrors that don't flatter. That's growth. Then life throws a trial you didn't ask for, and that's where your training gets tested.

Here's the strange part. You'll never feel ready, but you don't need to.

The point isn't to have the perfect spell prepared. The point is to show up with what you have, cast it with intention, and see what happens.

That way is the only means to discover what your magic is truly composed of.

What to Do With This

Start noticing what you're consuming. Ask yourself:

- Is this a scroll or a tome?
- Am I collecting knowledge or applying it?
- When was the last time I treated a moment like a trial instead of an inconvenience?

You don't need to go back and re-read everything you've ever highlighted. You just need to choose one idea and live it.

Let it stretch you.
Let it fail you.
Let it teach you something the page couldn't.

Your Initiate's Quest

Today, choose one idea you've "learned" before.

A quote, a belief, a truth you've heard so often you stopped thinking about it.

Then, test it in the real world.

- Speak up when you normally wouldn't.
- Sit in discomfort without rushing to fix it.
- Give grace when you're tempted to be right.

That's the trial.

You don't need to win. You just need to engage, because the real spell isn't the lesson.

It's what you do when it matters.

Input Is Incantation

"What you consume becomes your inner voice. Choose wisely what you let speak through you." — The Unknown Archmage

The Spell You Don't Know You're Casting

Not all magic looks like magic.

Some spells come in the form of headlines. Some sound like the scroll of a social feed or the looping rhythm of a song. Some are so subtle you don't even notice them until they're inside you, rewriting your thoughts, reshaping your expectations, and whispering ideas that never felt like yours to begin with.

Input is incantation.

Every piece of information you allow into your mind is a kind of spell, shaping how you feel, how you think, and even how you see the world.

As a Wizard, you're not just responsible for the spells you cast outward, but you are also responsible for the ones you let take root within.

Modern Spellcasting: The Noise Behind Your Eyes

Take a moment to think about what you've taken in today.

Podcasts, text threads, the news cycle, background TV, ads. Scroll after scroll after scroll. None of it feels heavy, but it builds, much like ash after fire, and here's what most people miss. Everything you consume has a cost.

It either builds your focus or scatters it.
It either deepens your insight or dulls your clarity.
It either amplifies your magic or clogs the channel.

This isn't about being "pure" or "positive." It's about being intentional.

The wrong input doesn't just waste your time. It shapes your internal narrative. It programs how you speak to yourself, what you believe about the world, and how you respond when life tests you.

If you fill your mind with garbage, don't be surprised when your magic misfires.

Stan Lee: A Legacy of Intentional Input

If anyone understood how powerful words and ideas can be, it was Stan Lee.

Alongside artists like Jack Kirby and Steve Ditko, he helped shape the Marvel Universe, not just as entertainment, but as a mirror. These stories weren't just entertainment, they became moral compasses, wrestling with themes like power, responsibility, identity, and belonging in ways comics rarely had before.

He was deeply aware that what people read shaped how they thought. That stories had the power to build empathy, challenge assumptions, and create meaning.

He didn't just write to entertain. He wrote to elevate.

Stan drew from mythology, philosophy, world events, and the quiet struggle of being human. He curated what he consumed and turned it into worlds that outlived him.

He once said, *"With great power comes great responsibility."*

It wasn't just a tagline. It was a worldview, and that worldview came from being intentional with input.

The Science of Input (and the Power of Choice)

Modern neuroscience tells us what Stan seemed to know intuitively. Your input becomes your wiring, that the brain is plastic, and it adapts based on repetition and experience, but here's what matters. Neuroplasticity doesn't just happen to you, you can direct it.

The more you consciously feed your mind certain inputs like music, language, habits of thought, the more your brain builds those neural pathways into default patterns.

- Expose yourself constantly to negativity? Your brain learns to expect it.
- Immerse yourself in creative thinking, gratitude, reflection? Your brain strengthens those capacities instead.

You're not just absorbing, you're training.

A famous study of London taxi drivers found they developed larger hippocampi, the part of the brain tied to spatial memory, after memorizing the city's maze-like streets (PNAS, 2000). Input literally reshapes brain structure.

It's not uniform. Individual differences matter like genetics, experiences, even trauma history influence how inputs are received. One person may spiral from stress, another may grow stronger. The key factor? Awareness and intentionality.

Even mindfulness, choosing where your attention goes, has been shown to override reactive pathways and rewire the brain (Journal of Neuroscience, 2011).

You can't control every input, but you can control what you keep.

Cleansing the Feed, Clearing the Mind

As a Wizard, part of your responsibility is protecting the inner sanctum of your mind.

That means taking inventory, not just of what you're thinking… but where those thoughts came from.

Ask yourself:

- What am I regularly watching, listening to, reading?
- How does it make me feel?
- Who am I becoming as a result?

Would you cast the kinds of thoughts you've been repeating lately on someone you love?

If not, then it's time for a cleansing spell.

Not dramatic.
Not a digital purge.
Just a simple, sacred boundary:

"I don't let everything into the tower."

Choose Your Incantations with Care

The most powerful Wizards don't just protect their minds, they feed them intentionally.

You can do the same.

Start small:

- Create a morning playlist that lifts your energy.
- Follow creators who challenge you in meaningful ways.
- Read one page of a book that reminds you of your potential.
- Have a quiet moment without input and let your own thoughts echo.

You're not just consuming content. You're crafting your mental spellbook.

Make sure what's going in is worthy of coming back out.

Your Initiate's Quest

For the next three days, perform an Input Audit.

1. Notice what you're consuming. Social media, conversations, music, podcasts, news.
2. Reflect on how each one makes you feel afterward.
3. Replace one toxic or draining input with something that nurtures clarity, insight, or peace.

Ask yourself:

"What am I giving my mind permission to carry?"

What you carry becomes what you cast.

And what you cast becomes your world.

Cursebreaking

> *"Some curses are not cast. They are passed down. The Wizard's task is not to hate them, but to unbind them."*
> — The Unknown Archmage

Not All Spells Are Yours

There are spells you cast on purpose, and then there are the ones you carry without realizing until the weight starts to pull you down. These are the inherited spells that are passed silently, reinforced quietly. They don't come with a villain or a villain's lair. They come with a smile. A shrug, or a "that's just how it is."

These spells are better known as curses.

Not curses in the fairy tale sense but patterns, beliefs, and self-perceptions that you didn't choose… but that have shaped you all the same and before you can break them, you have to be willing to see them.

The Nature of a Curse

Curses aren't always obvious. They're not always trauma or tragedy. Sometimes, they're just phrases you've heard so many times they etched themselves into your mind:

"We don't talk about that."
"That's just how you are."
"You're the responsible one."
"People like us don't do things like that."
"Why would you want more?"

These aren't evil, but they are limiting, and when you act on them long enough, they begin to shape your identity. Not because they're true... but because they're familiar.

That's what makes them dangerous.

Signs You're Under a Curse

How do you know if a belief or behavior is really a curse?

Start here:

- You keep repeating a pattern that doesn't serve you, even though you know better.
- You feel resistance, fear, or guilt around certain types of success or expression.
- You shrink around certain people or environments without understanding why.
- You have internal reactions that feel bigger than the moment.

These are clues.

Not proof of weakness, proof that something has been operating underneath your awareness.

This is when you realize you've been under someone else's spell.

A Familiar Role, A Quiet Curse

I once heard someone describe their curse like this, and it's stayed with me ever since.

They were a middle child, and like many middle children, they learned early how to disappear into the space between louder voices. They became the mediator, the peacemaker, the one who smoothed things over. It made them feel useful,even strong, but as they grew older, they realized something quietly devastating. They had become the person who fixed everyone else's problems... and never thought to fix their own.

They apologized for things that weren't theirs.
They stepped in to calm tension, even when the conflict had nothing to do with them.
They buried their own needs, convinced that to need anything was to cause conflict.

That was the curse, the belief that peace only existed if they held it for everyone else, and yet, something changed. They began to notice the pattern, to speak about their own needs, to catch the apology mid-breath and ask, "Do I really need to carry this?"

They didn't reject the part of them that wanted to help others. They just stopped sacrificing themselves to do it. Some curses are heavy and others disguise themselves as kindness.

Either way, once you see the pattern, you can choose what to keep and what to unbind.

Real-World Magic

Actor and storyteller Viola Davis has spoken openly about the long shadow cast by her early life growing up in poverty, facing racism, being told what she could or couldn't become.

For years, the scripts she was offered told her she was limited. That she could only play certain roles, that her worth had borders, but she didn't accept those scripts. She rewrote them.

Her career is a public act of cursebreaking.

She didn't just escape her story, she claimed it, and in doing so, she created space for thousands of others to see themselves reflected in her strength, her presence, her voice.

That's the power of naming a curse and choosing to unbind it.

Cursebreaking Requires Consciousness

You can't break a curse you won't name. You can't unbind what you're still pretending fits.

This is slow magic, but it's lasting.

Cursebreaking doesn't mean rejecting your past.
It means choosing not to repeat what's no longer true.
It means meeting the belief, looking it in the eye, and saying, "You got me this far. But you don't get to shape the rest."

How to Break a Curse

1. **Name it** - What belief, behavior, or story are you carrying that don't serve the Wizard you're becoming?

2. **Trace it** - Where did it come from? Was it taught? Modeled? Rewarded? Was it ever even yours?

3. **Replace it** - What spell would you rather cast? What truth feels more aligned, even if it's unfamiliar?

You don't have to feel ready, you just have to be willing.

The Cursebreaker's Responsibility

Breaking a curse doesn't mean you owe anyone an explanation, but you owe yourself the space to live unbound, and when you do? When you start walking without that weight? Others will notice, and without even trying, you'll show them they can break their own.

Your Initiate's Quest

Reflect and journal:

- What belief or behavior am I carrying that may have been passed down, not chosen?
- What part of me is still operating under someone else's spell?
- What would it mean to break that cycle, not with fire, but with clarity?

Then, write a new incantation. One that reflects the truth you choose now, because the most powerful spells aren't the ones you cast at others.

They're the ones you stop casting at yourself.

The Arcane Identity

Who Told You Who You Are?

Before you had language, you were already being named. Some labels were small: smart, lazy, funny, sensitive. Some were heavier: too much, not enough, troublemaker, peacemaker, problem, perfectionist.

None of them came from you.

Family, teachers, culture, and systems passed them down, speaking them over you. Like any good spell, the more they were repeated, the more power they held. You may not remember when the naming happened, but you've felt its weight.

That's the thing about identity. It's often built long before you realize you're the one living inside it, and the longer you wear the spell, the harder it is to see it's not actually you.

Identity Is a Spell

Let's be clear. Identity isn't just who you are. It's who you've been *told* you are, and who you've come to *believe* you are.

We build beliefs the same way we build spells.

Written through experience
Spoken aloud through repetition
Reinforced by attention
Strengthened by emotion

Think of the things you say about yourself without even thinking.

"I'm bad at finishing things."
"I've always been shy."
"I'm terrible with money."
"I'm not creative."
"That's just how I am."

Each of those is a **binding spell,** not because it's "bad" but because it becomes **truth through repetition.**

This is the magic of identity, and the trap, because once you believe the spell, your actions align with it. You make choices that reinforce it. You attract people who reflect it back to you, and before long, the idea becomes the *evidence.*

The Shadow in the Mirror

What makes identity so tricky is that it doesn't always feel harmful.

Sometimes it *feels like home.*

Even if it's small, even if it hurts, because it's familiar. Therefore, people often resist change, not because they can't do it, but because the new self feels *unfamiliar,* unstable, unproven. Even pain can be safe if it's what you know.

This is especially true for those walking a fresh path.

The person stepping into leadership who still hears "you're not responsible enough."
The artist trying to create while carrying the belief "you're not original."
The healer who still sees themselves as broken.

When you cast a new identity spell, one that says "I am growing," "I am creative," "I am powerful", your **old identity reacts.**

It says, *"Who do you think you are?"*

That's not a flaw.
That's the spell fraying.
That's the mirror cracking.

That's the moment you keep going.

Brandon Sanderson: The Rewrite Wizard

If anyone understands what it means to cast a new identity spell, its fantasy author **Brandon Sanderson**.

Early in his career, he didn't look or sound like what people expected a successful writer to be. He was quiet, thoughtful, obsessed with world building. He was also awkward in interviews, and for years, he was rejected. Over and over, he was told directly or indirectly that he wasn't "marketable," but instead of chasing someone else's image of success, Brandon did something much more powerful. He kept writing.

He wrote book after book, fifteen of them before one was finally accepted for publication. He leaned into his identity as a builder of intricate, layered magic systems. He trusted that his voice didn't need to sound like everyone else's. He stopped asking for permission and started creating on his own terms.

Now? He's one of the most prolific fantasy authors alive, and when the publishing world said "you can't do that," he quietly raised over $40 million in one of the most successful independent publishing campaigns in history. He didn't wait to be named a Wizard. He became one, word by word.

That's arcane identity.

Building the New Spell

So what does it take to rewrite your own identity spell? You don't need to burn everything down and you don't need to reinvent yourself overnight. You just need to *choose a new incantation.*

Start with what you say about yourself.
"I'm learning to be more present."
"I'm becoming someone who finishes."
"I'm not the same person I was last year."
These are soft spells, gentle ones, but they're no less powerful. Then, surround yourself with new mirrors, people who reflect the version of you you're stepping into. Not because you need validation, but because your environment is part of your spellwork. Even your space matters.

What's on your walls.
What's on your shelves.
What's in your ears.

Make it match who you're becoming. Speak the new spell.

Write it.
Live it.

Let it feel awkward at first, it should.

You're not faking, you're forging.

Resistance Is the Test

Here's the part no one tells you. The more powerful the identity you're stepping into, the more resistance you'll feel. That doesn't mean it's wrong, that means it's *working*. Your nervous system, your subconscious, your old identity, they'll all try to "protect" you from change. That's what they've been trained to do.

The Initiate knows. Resistance is not the enemy, it's the echo of who you used to be... trying to hold the tower. Thank it and keep going.

You Are Already Becoming

The Arcane Identity isn't about *becoming someone else.* It's about stripping away the false spells. The names you didn't choose, the limits you inherited, the roles you were cast in without audition. You don't need to build something from nothing, you just need to return to what was already there, beneath the layers.

You are not who they named you. You are who you are becoming.

Your Initiate's Quest

Journal prompts:

- What part of your identity was assigned to you, not chosen?
- What do you say about yourself that might actually be a spell you didn't write?
- What truth do you want to cast moving forward?

Optional incantation:

"I am becoming the version of me I was always meant to meet."

If it feels right, write your Wizard name. Not for the world, not for show, but as a quiet claim of the self you're growing into.

A name that calls power forward.
A name that speaks to your becoming.

Even Wizards Need Rest

"Even the stars retreat beyond the veil. So must you."
— The Unknown Archmage

The Silence After the Spell

Not every lesson crackles with light. Some arrive like a slow breath, a still room, a body that finally exhales. There comes a time in every Wizard's path when the rituals are familiar, the books are open, and the wand is warm… but nothing flows.

Not because you've forgotten the magic, but because you've forgotten to *rest*.

Modern spellcasting often masquerades as productivity, ambition, and endless output. It teaches us that more is always better. That stopping means falling behind. That stillness is stagnation, but experienced Wizards know better. They know that casting without rest doesn't make you powerful.

It makes you brittle.

Why We Resist the Pause

We fear what might surface in the quiet. We're taught that our worth is measured in usefulness, how much we do, how much we give, how much we can push through without cracking.

We associate movement with progress, and when we stop, a voice whispers, *You're lazy. You're weak. You're falling behind,* but that voice isn't your intuition. It's your programming.

It's the echo of a culture that's forgotten its own rhythm. A system that demands spells without ever teaching recovery, a belief that says, "Keep casting, don't question, don't breathe."

You can resist it. You *must* resist it, because the more powerful the magic, the more rest it requires to hold.

The Alchemy of Recovery

True magic doesn't just live in movement, it lives in what happens *after* the movement ends. Rest isn't idle for a Wizard's mind. It's when the subconscious sorts the arcane from the trivial, and neuroscience has begun to reveal what Wizards have long sensed. The mind needs space to integrate what it learns. When you're not focused on a task, like walking, daydreaming, or simply staring into nothing, your brain shifts into what's known as the **Default Mode Network** (DMN). This isn't wasted time. It's a vital activity.

The DMN supports:

Self-reflection
Abstract thinking
Creativity
Memory consolidation

Therefore, breakthrough ideas often surface during mundane tasks. What feels like "doing nothing" is actually arcane incubation.

Meanwhile, REM sleep activates the brain's emotional and memory centers, replaying the day's events at speeds up to 20x normal (Nature, 2019). It doesn't just log your experiences; it edits them, weaving your insights into the deeper fabric of your understanding.

And Stage 2 NREM sleep strengthens your working memory, the foundation of complex thought and problem-solving (Journal of Sleep Research, 2020).

You're not just resting.

You're rewriting your inner architecture.
You're upgrading your spellbook.
Skipping rest to "work harder" isn't discipline.

It's spell sabotage.

A Wizard who honors rest doesn't fall behind. They move forward with less friction and more precision.

The Wizard Who Waits to Return

In a world that rewards constant output, few creators choose silence. Fewer still choose it with purpose. **Claudio Sanchez** is one of them.

The visionary behind *Coheed and Cambria* and *The Amory Wars* mythos, Claudio doesn't just release music, he crafts entire worlds. His albums aren't just concept records, they are time capsules. Each riff, each lyric, each character is part of a decades-long chronicle, and yet, Claudio doesn't chase content. He retreats. Not into full isolation, he may appear at a con, drop a side project, speak in interviews, but always with a sense of distance from the noise.

He steps away from the spotlight, not to disappear, but to *listen* to the story's demands. Between releases, he allows space. Time to imagine, time to rebuild. His returns don't follow trends, they follow alignment.

His process reflects what psychologists call "incubation," the creative phase where stepping away from the work allows deeper ideas to take shape (Journal of Creative Behavior, 2018).

Claudio lets ideas *simmer* until they're ready, not until they're scheduled. His albums aren't just spells, they're rituals released when the story says it's time. He reminds us that magic isn't always about momentum. Sometimes, it's about patience, silence, deep creative trust, and that's what makes him a true Wizard. Not the complexity of the world he builds, but the wisdom to know when to *pause between the realms.*

The Cost of Ignoring the Call

When you ignore your body's request for rest, it doesn't whisper.

It starts to scream. Irritability, brain fog, emotional collapse, physical fatigue that sleep can't fix. You're not lazy. You're empty, and here's the most dangerous part. You can *still function* like that. You can go weeks, months, even years in survival mode. Casting spells on fumes. Performing power instead of embodying it.

Until the moment you break.

Burnout doesn't feel dramatic. It feels numb, detached, like watching your own life through fogged glass, but when you rest, really rest, you remember who you are.

Recovery Is Ritual

Rest isn't just sleep. It's space.

Unstructured time
Solitude
Play
Reflection
Stillness
Nature
Sacred boredom

This isn't luxury, it's spell preparation. Think of it as charging your wand, clearing your arcane circuitry, tuning your internal resonance.

Rituals of rest:

A walk without headphones
A day with no agenda
A journal with no goals
Music and tea
Silence

You don't rest to earn more productivity. You rest to remember your magic.

Boundaries Are a Wizard's Circle

Every powerful Wizard draws a circle, not to push others away, but to protect what's within.

Rest *requires* boundaries:

Saying no

Logging off
Leaving the scroll unopened
Letting the spellbook stay closed
This isn't selfish, it's sacred. You cannot cast clean spells from a cluttered soul. Protecting your energy is not weakness.

It's wisdom.

The Myth of Endless Casting

In every story, there's a Wizard who tries to cast one spell too many. They know they're spent. They feel the fray. But the moment is urgent. The need is great. And so they whisper: *Just one more spell,* and then something breaks.

In stories, this makes for drama. In life? It leads to collapse.

You're not a story arc. You're not a machine. You are a living conduit of energy and will, and you are meant to be well. Wizards don't prove their power through exhaustion. They prove it by knowing when to rest.

They prove it by knowing *when to stop.*

Initiate's Quest

Take the next three days to design your Rest Ritual.

Choose one moment each day where you will *do nothing with intention.*

A walk
A nap
A blank page
Music and tea
Silence

Notice what rises in the stillness and repeat.

Ask yourself:

What am I afraid will happen if I rest?
What has rest already healed in me before?

The Final Reflection: Becoming the Initiate

If you've made it this far, you've walked through fire, fog, and your own shadow.

You began as **The Apprentice** - Curious, uncertain, eager to learn. You answered the Call. You opened your blank spellbook. You dared to try.

You became **The Novice** - Building routines, managing your energy, learning how to wield your focus and recover from your misfires.

Now, you've walked the path of **The Initiate** - the one who steps inward.

You've explored wisdom, identity, input, and inner architecture, and here, in this final chapter, you've reclaimed the sacred art of *stopping*. You've learned that a Wizard gathers not only knowledge. A Wizard *gathers themselves,* and now… something stirs.

You feel it, don't you?

The next threshold calls. But not with noise or fire. With stillness, with clarity, with presence. You are not the same as when you began.

You are no longer casting to be seen. You are casting to become.

The Adept does not need louder spells. They need deeper silence.

IV

The Adept

You've stopped reaching for the robe.

You wear it now.

The Adept stage is quiet confidence. Fewer words, deeper spells. You no longer chase every spell, you choose the ones that matter. You've learned to budget your energy, sharpen your focus, and lead with no need to be loud.

You aren't proving yourself anymore. You're practicing power with precision.

This isn't where the learning ends. But it's where self-trust begins.

From Apprentice to Archmage

> **"Mastery wears no robe, bears no ring, only the weight of what moves when no one is watching."**
> — The Unknown Archmage

The Moment Between

There's a space you rarely notice when you're in it. It doesn't come with applause, or arrive with a robe and a title. It's the quiet moment when you realize you no longer need to prove you're a Wizard.

You simply are one.

Not because the world told you, but because you've been living like it, spell by spell, day by day, choice by choice. That's where the Adept begins. Not in more ambition, but in recognition.

Not because you've finished growing, but because you've begun growing with *intention.* You are no longer casting just to become someone. You are casting because you *already are.*

This is the shift. It doesn't feel loud, but it feels true.

The Spiral Path

If the Apprentice learns by reaching outward, the Adept learns by looking inward and seeing the pattern that's always been there.

Growth is not a line. It is a spiral.

You return to the same themes, focus, identity, self-worth, but now you meet them from a different place. With more stillness and more trust. You don't dodge discomfort anymore, you greet it. You don't resist the pause, you now understand it is part of the rhythm. The fear didn't vanish, but it no longer writes your decisions.

The doubt still whispers, but it no longer decides when you speak. You've learned that power doesn't mean more effort, it just means less friction, fewer misfires, and more aligned movement.

The spiral brings you back to what you thought you understood and shows you how far you've truly come.

The Mirror and the Weight

There is a moment, usually small, always real, when you glimpse who you've become.

It could be in your reflection.
It could be in a sentence you speak surprises even you.
It could be in how someone else looks at you differently, quietly, with respect they don't name.

In that moment, you realize you've changed. Not into someone else, but into someone *whole.* You remember the Apprentice who opened this book, curious, cautious, hoping there was something more inside. You remember the Novice who built rituals from scratch and misfired anyway. You remember the Initiate who unlearned the false names, cracked open the old identity spells, and sat in the silence, and now?

Now you walk differently. Your rituals don't need ceremony, your spellbook isn't carried, it's lived, your presence has become your proof. You don't move louder.

You move *truer*.

You Are Becoming Someone's Archmage

Here is the part that sneaks up on you. While you've been walking, someone else has been watching. Not because they think you have all the answers, but because you've walked with integrity, because you didn't quit when it got quiet, because you didn't wait to be perfect before you acted.

They may not tell you, they may not even know how to name it, but you are becoming their Archmage. Not with declarations, but with presence, with steadiness, with the way you carry your magic like breath, not as performance, but as truth.

This is not about being above anyone. It is about becoming someone who shows what's possible.

The robe doesn't make the Archmage. The responsibility does, and it's already forming around you.

The Adept's Call

You don't need a lesson now. You need a moment of acknowledgment.

Pause.

Reflect.

Not on what you want next, but on what you've already done.

Ask yourself:

What once felt impossible that now feels integrated?
What have you unlearned that gave you your strength back?
Where do you move with clarity now, where before there was only reaction?

Then write to the Apprentice within you.

Let them know they weren't wrong to believe.
Let them know the magic was real.
Let them know *you became the one they hoped you could be.*

Not because of one moment, but because of many. Not because of what you knew, but because of what you chose again and again.

You are not the Archmage yet, but now, when you reach for the wand, you do not hesitate, and that changes everything.

Teach the Next Wizard

"To teach is to hold the torch, not for attention, but so someone else can see the path."
— The Unknown Archmage

The Shift

There is a moment in every Wizard's journey when the question changes. It is no longer; *What else can I learn?* It becomes; *What can I give?* Not because your learning is done, but because what you've learned now wants to be passed on.

You don't teach because you're finished. You teach because the path is still warm beneath your feet and others are just now stepping onto it.

This is the quiet transition from Adept to something more.

Not louder.
Not holier.
But deeper.

You Are Already Teaching

You may not realize it, but someone is already watching the way you move. They're noticing how you hold your focus, how you recover from mistakes, or how you treat your energy, your craft, your mind, and they're learning.

Not from your words, but from your *being*.

You may never see their face, but you are already shaping someone's idea of what it looks like living with clarity.

This is the beginning of a legacy.

Teaching Without Ego

Real teaching doesn't demand applause. It doesn't need disciples. It doesn't rely on hierarchy.

It requires space, presence, and knowing when to step forward or when to step aside.

A true Wizard does not create followers. They awaken *other Wizards.*

To teach is not to say, *"Do as I do."* It is to ask, *"What in you is waiting to rise?"*

Bob Ross: The Wizard of Permission

Bob Ross didn't just teach people to paint. He taught people to be *gentle with themselves.* To try, even to mess up, but always to keep going. He didn't demand perfection, and he didn't gatekeep technique. He offered a steady voice, a calm rhythm, and the radical spell of encouragement. His famous line *"We don't make mistakes, just happy little accidents"* was more than charm. It was a transformation.

Bob Ross gave people access to something sacred, creative self-trust.

That's teaching, and that's Wizardry.

Steve Irwin: The Wizard of Passion

Steve Irwin taught through fire, joyful, wild, fearless energy. He didn't read facts from a card; he *embodied* the love he wanted others to feel. His enthusiasm wasn't a performance. It was permission, permission to love what others feared, to protect what others ignored, to feel *deeply* in a world that tries to stay cool and detached.

He didn't just teach wildlife. He taught wonder, and wonder, when offered freely, is a spell that never stops echoing.

Keanu Reeves: The Wizard of Presence

Keanu Reeves rarely calls attention to himself, but people pay attention anyway. He moves with grace, listens before speaking, and he creates space wherever he goes. He doesn't preach wisdom, but his restraint teaches it. He doesn't ask for reverence, but his humility commands it.

He is a Wizard of quiet power.

A reminder that how you move through the world teaches others more than any lecture ever could, and that's the deeper truth. You are always teaching.

The only question left is, what are you passing on?

Legacy as Living Spellwork

Teaching is not about arriving. It's about opening the door behind you.

It's not about having all the answers. It's about creating space for others to find their own. You don't need a platform to teach and you don't need permission.

You only need to embody your magic visibly enough for someone else to recognize their own.

That's how the lineage continues.
That's how the magic survives.
That's how we make sure the next wizard has something to rise into.

The Adept's Call

Your quest is not to create a classroom. It is to become a living scroll.

Reflect:
What do you wish someone had told you earlier?
What have you learned through trial that you now carry as truth?
Who in your life might be watching, waiting for permission to believe in themselves?

Then write this:

Your first teaching spell.

One sentence. A truth, a moment of clarity that cost you something to earn.

Offer it.

Even if no one hears it yet. Even if you're not sure it's perfect. Teaching begins with the offering, not the outcome. You do not need to be the Archmage to teach. You need only be someone who has walked the path and is willing to turn and extend your hand. The next Wizard is already watching.

Light the torch, and leave the path lit behind you.

Build Your Tower

"The world will not give you space to become. You must build it."
— The Unknown Archmage

The Tower Is Claimed, Not Given

There comes a point when knowledge alone is no longer enough. Not because you've learned everything, but because your magic needs a place to live.

By now, you've gathered tools, rituals, the awareness. You've seen the misfires, and you've begun casting with clarity, but clarity doesn't last without *structure*.

Without a place to return to, without something sacred you've chosen to protect. The Tower is not a symbol.

It's a necessity.
It's not a retreat.
It's an anchor.

The world will not offer it to you. You will have to build it yourself.

Why Wizards Need Towers

Without a Tower, you become reactive.

You answer every call, open every scroll, absorb every urgency that isn't yours. You try to cast spells in rooms that aren't safe, in rhythms that aren't yours, on timelines that were never designed for magic. You wonder why it feels fractured, and it's the Tower that changes that.

It is space reclaimed.
It is rhythm restored.
It is sovereignty made structural.

It may be physical. It may be energetic. But it always says the same thing: *"This is mine, and this is where I remember who I am."*

A Memory from the Wandering Years

Growing up, space was rare.

Not physical space, always, but something deeper. The space where your thoughts could echo, where your own voice could rise without interruption. Where you could just be.

It never lasted long. A few stolen minutes, a quiet hallway, a flicker of solitude before the next demand arrived, but something changed when I turned sixteen.

I got my driver's license.

The car was a hand-me-down, and it was nothing special. My sister had driven it before me. It didn't sparkle, but it was *mine*. So I cleaned it, installed speakers, and made playlists. I lit candles in my mind and called it sacred, and then I did what no one could stop me from doing.

I drove.

I didn't go anywhere, and that wasn't the point. I drove just to *be*, to listen, to think, to feel, to remember myself. That car became my tower before I had the words for it.

I wasn't hiding. I was rebuilding. The world outside blurred, the music shaped the air, and something in me settled. I didn't know it then, but I was already practicing spellwork.

Ritual.
Silence.
Sovereignty.

That's the thing about Towers. Sometimes you don't recognize them until much later, but they're always waiting to be built again.

The Architecture of Alignment

Towers are not always made of stone. But they are always made of *intention*.

Ask yourself:

Where do I think most clearly?
What helps me remember myself?
What pattern, environment, or ritual brings me back into resonance?

Your Tower may be a room, a corner, a drive or even a stretch of silence.

It may be:

A desk you keep clean
A walk you never skip
A song you play before creating
A journal that only you read
A time of day no one else can claim

It isn't about grandeur. It's about *gravity.* Something that pulls you back to your center every time you begin to float.

Boundaries Are the Gates

A Tower is not sacred because it exists. It's sacred because of what you don't allow inside.

You must choose:

What voices stay out
What hours are untouchable
What energy no longer gets a key

This is not selfish, this is spellcraft. A Wizard without boundaries is a leaking cauldron, always pouring, never full.

The Tower becomes the place where your energy gathers again.

Not to hoard it, but to offer it on your terms.

The Adept's Call

You've earned the right to protect your clarity.

Your quest:

1. Name your Tower.
2. It might be a space. A practice. A ritual. A rhythm.
3. Wherever you feel most like yourself, honor it. Claim it.
4. Reinforce the Gate.
5. Choose one boundary you've been avoiding. A space or time you need to protect.
6. Draw the circle. Keep it sacred.
7. Return.
8. This week, enter your tower on purpose.
9. Even if just for ten minutes. Sit in the silence.
10. Let yourself arrive.

Because the spell doesn't begin when you speak.

It begins when you return to the place that lets your voice rise true.

Spell Economy

The Power Is Not Free

The deeper into the path you go, the more you realize, not every spell should be cast.

In the beginning, you try everything. You say yes to every opportunity; you burn the candle, not just at both ends, but from the middle too. You confuse motion with progress. Casting with mastery, but mastery isn't more magic. It's smarter magic.

A Wizard doesn't flex by flinging fireballs at every problem. A true Wizard studies the situation, gauges the risk, chooses the spell that does *exactly enough*, and nothing more.

Welcome to Spell Economy.

It's not about doing less. It's about doing wisely. It's about recognizing your mana is not infinite, even if your potential is. The adept stage is where you

141

stop proving and start practicing power with precision. Every yes is a spell. Every focus is a cost. Every choice has consequences.

It's time to learn how to spend your magic like it matters.

The Cost of Casting

We talk a lot about casting spells, but here's something real: every spell drains you. Focus, energy, time, emotional labor, it all adds up. If you're not careful, you go broke, and just like a new player spamming spells until they're out of mana , you can't heal the party when it counts. Real life works the same way. You can blow all your energy on tasks that look urgent but aren't meaningful, and then when the big moment comes, you've got nothing left to give.

This chapter is about *not* letting that happen.

To use your magic well, you need to:

Know what you're actually casting.
Know what it costs.
Decide if it's worth it.

If you can't answer those three questions, you're not in control of your spell economy.

You're reacting, and not responding.

The Spells That Drain You Most

Not all spells cost the same. Some feel small but are mana monsters under the surface. Here are a few to look out for:

Over-Explaining: The urge to justify yourself to everyone, especially people who don't actually care. High mana cost. Low return.

Constant Context Switching: Jumping from tab to tab, task to task, convo to convo. Each switch has a cost. Fragmented attention is fragmented power.

Unclear Goals: Working hard on things you haven't actually defined. The spell never finishes. You just keep pouring mana into a bottomless ritual.

Emotional Labor: Managing everyone else's reactions before your own needs. Trying to be liked, understood, or validated by people who are not your party.

Trying to Prove You Belong: This one is sneaky. It wears different hats, perfectionism, overwork, imposter syndrome. The cost? All of it.

These aren't terrible spells. They're just expensive. And if you're casting them by default, you're burning energy that could go elsewhere.

The Spells That Pay You Back

Some spells *generate* mana. They restore, replenish, empower. These are your renewables. Learn what yours are and protect them at all costs.

Deep Work: Getting lost in the zone on something that aligns with your purpose. This is high-cost, high-reward casting. Worth it.

Connection: Real connection. Not small talk, not networking. But those "I see you" moments. They refill your mana faster than rest alone.

Rituals: Any consistent act that grounds you. Doesn't need to be big. Could be journaling, walking, reading, or just drinking your coffee in silence.

Creative Expression: Writing, building, making something that didn't exist before. Especially when no one's watching.

Learning Something That Sparks You: Not for a resume. For you. Because curiosity is its own kind of mana.

When you build your day around these, the whole economy shifts. You stop living in deficit, and you grow your reserves.

Real Wizards Budget

Mana budgeting is real. You wake up with a certain amount of energy, emotional, physical, mental, and how you spend it? That's the spell economy.

Try this:

Track your mana leaks for a day. Every time you feel drained, ask:

What just cost me?
Did I choose to spend that?
Did it move me closer to my mission?

Name your high-value spells. These are the things that make everything else easier. Protect them.

Choose your daily spell limit, not because you're weak, but because you're wise.

This isn't a restriction. This is resource management.

You're not here to be busy. You're here to cast with intention.

Scarcity vs Strategy

Some people live in scarcity:

"I have to say yes."
"I can't afford to rest."
"If I don't do it, no one will."

Adept Wizards live in strategy:

"Not every spell is mine to cast."
"Rest is how I refine my power."
"My no makes space for my strongest yes."

This shift is everything, because when you stop casting out of fear and start casting from focus, you stop wasting your magic.

You start shaping reality.

Mana Mastery = Self Trust

The deeper truth of spell economy is this. You have to trust yourself to stop, believe the work will still be there, and believe your value isn't tied to how much you produce.

A Wizard doesn't cast all day to prove they're powerful. They cast once, with precision, and the whole room changes.

You want to live like a Wizard? Start by asking, not just "What can I do today?" but "What's the one spell that actually matters?"

Cast that.
Then recover.

Then return.

A real Wizard doesn't waste, they wield.

The Adept's Call: Practice Your Spell Economy

You've read the ideas, now let's make them real. Pick one of the following or try them all.

The goal is clarity, not perfection.

Track Your Mana Leaks for 3 Days

Keep a simple log. Every time you feel drained, frustrated, or foggy, write what you were doing. Label it as: *Renewing, Neutral,* or *Draining.* Patterns will emerge.
Audit Your Spellbook

List your current commitments. For each one, ask:

What spell is this?
What does it cost?
Is the outcome worth the mana?

If it's not aligned or returning value, it may be time to release it.

Create a High-Value Spell List

Write down 5 activities that reliably replenish your energy or momentum. Post it somewhere visible. When you feel off, cast one of those spells.
Choose a Daily Limit
Give yourself a cap. "Three major casts a day." Or "90 minutes of deep work max." Don't see it as a ceiling. See it as smart spell prep.

This is how you stop living in reaction. This is how you cast like an Adept.

The Wizard in the Mirror

> **"A mirror shows what you are. A Wizard sees what they're becoming."**
> — The Unknown Archmage

The Moment You See It

There's a moment every real Wizard hits. A moment that sneaks up on you. You're brushing your teeth, walking the dog, sitting in a meeting, and the world is normal. You're just doing the day and then something clicks.

You hear yourself speak.
You make a decision without panic.
You notice a pattern you used to miss, and suddenly, there it is. *You've changed.*

The person in the mirror isn't who you used to be. They're more calm, more thoughtful, more capable. More… Wizard.

Not because you finally got a title or trophy, but because you're seeing the truth.

You're not pretending anymore. You're just becoming.

The Mirror as a Test

We think tests are big moments. Job interviews, final exams, D&D boss fights, but one of the real tests? Is the mirror.

When the noise quiets, when the show is over, when it's just you and your reflection, what do you see?

A Wizard doesn't flinch there. They don't need applause, or proof, they recognize themselves. Even when it's quiet, even when no one else is watching.

That's the true test of the Adept, not just what you can do, but who you've become while doing it.

My Reflection Was Late to Arrive

Most of us have felt this at some point. *Am I just pretending to know what I'm doing?* I shouldn't be in charge of this. I'm not qualified. Someone's going to figure out I do not know what I'm doing.

That feeling? It stuck with me for a long time.

Through jobs, through projects, through roles I earned but didn't believe I deserved. I would go to work, do my best, and still leave wondering: *was that good enough? Or was I just lucky again?*

Spoiler: I was good. I just hadn't seen myself yet.

It took years of practice, reflection, and some big personal shifts to finally catch my progress. One of the biggest shifts? Becoming a parent.

Parenthood is its own kind of magic. It is wild, messy, unscripted, and like most people, I didn't feel ready. I kept comparing myself to my own parents, thinking; *They knew what they were doing. They had it together.*

Over time, I realized something quietly powerful. They didn't have it all figured out either. They just kept showing up. They learned as they went, and now, as I watch my own child grow and become their own person, I see it. I'm not faking it. I'm walking the path, just like they did.

That's when the mirror changed for me. That's when I stopped seeing a fraud and started seeing the Wizard.

The Shadow Side

Here's what most books skip. Wizards have a shadow side.

The more you know, the more your ego wants to talk. The better you get, the more you can look down.

Power can twist.

When you hit the Adept phase, it's easy to fall into the trap of judgment. To forget what it felt like to be the beginner, to believe your way is the way.

The antidote? Humility.
The spell? Remembering you're always learning.

Even Archmages don't know everything. They just know how to ask better questions.

When you look in the mirror, don't just ask, *How strong am I?* Ask, *how am I using that strength?*

What the Mirror Reveals

The mirror doesn't lie. It reflects. And if you've been doing the work, the rituals, the learning, the showing up when no one claps, then it's time to stop pretending you're still at level one.

You're not.

The spells are landing. The tower is forming. You've learned your rhythm, and now?

You have power.
You have influence.
You have choices.

What the mirror reveals isn't perfection. It's a presence, it's ownership, and it's you choosing who to be next.

The Adept's Call: See the Wizard

Time to meet yourself where you are.

1. **Mirror Check-In**
   Look at yourself, not to recite anything, but to *observe*. What's changed in how you carry yourself? What energy do you bring into the room now that you didn't before?

2. **Write Your Wizard Snapshot**
   In your spellbook or journal, list 5 clear ways you've grown since starting this path. Not vague ideas, specific changes. What habits have shifted? What mindsets have evolved?

3. **Define Your Current Spell**

What's the primary spell you cast right now? Is it building something? Supporting others? Saying no? Leading? Teaching? Define it clearly and name it.

4. **Example**:

- *The Spell of Holding Boundaries*
- *The Spell of Teaching with Patience*
- *The Spell of Quiet Confidence*

The name matters less than the clarity. This is your current identity in action.

The End of the Adept

You've studied the scrolls, learned your limits, chosen your spells. You've built rituals, you budgeted mana, practiced power with precision, and you've stopped casting for applause. You've started casting with clarity.

This is the turning point.

You don't need more theory, you just need integration. The next level isn't about learning more, it's about becoming more. Not by doing different things, but by doing them as someone who knows who they are.

This is the end of the Adept.

The robes no longer feel borrowed. The wand fits your hand. And the tower you thought belonged to someone else? You've already built the foundation.

Look in the mirror.
The Wizard is you.
Turn the page.

It's time to become the Archmage.

V

The Archmage

You don't need a title.

The Archmage doesn't walk in with fanfare. They arrive like weather, steady, inevitable, grounded.

This phase is integration. The wisdom behind the wand. The silence between the spells. You no longer need to be seen to know your power. You no longer cast to impress. You cast to serve.

The Archmage is not above the journey. They are the journey, living proof of what it looks like to walk it fully.

This part isn't about the next goal. It's about what remains after the fire, the tests, and the noise.

It's what you choose to leave behind.

The Final Spell

You've come far.

Not just through this book, but through yourself. You've questioned, practiced, stumbled, adapted. You've learned that magic isn't a force you summon from the sky, it's the way you meet your life. The questions you ask. The energy you protect. The stories you rewrite. Every part of this journey has been preparing you for what's next.

What comes next doesn't live in a paragraph. It isn't something I can teach. That's the nature of a final spell. I can't hand it to you. It has to be cast.

There comes a moment in every Wizard's journey when the scrolls end. When the diagrams fade, when the teacher steps back, not because the learning is over, but because the learning has taken root. The path continues, but it no longer needs to be described. It must be walked.

This chapter doesn't offer new tactics.
It doesn't introduce a spell or a practice.

It does something more sacred. It recognizes the shift.

The one you already feel.

The one where the Wizard stops gathering and starts giving. They stop asking what the magic is and realizes; they *are* the magic now.

That's what the final spell is. It's not a fireball, not a secret ritual, but the decision to stop seeking power and begin shaping the world with what you've already learned. It's the quiet confidence that arises not from knowing everything, but from choosing to act with what you *do* know, even when no one is watching.

You may not feel ready and that's fine. Most Archmages never do, but readiness was never the requirement. What matters now isn't certainty, its presence, its return, it's the choice to keep showing up with intention, even when the spark is dim, even when the outcome is unknown.

That's the difference between the student and the Archmage. The student hopes the spell will work. The Archmage shows up and casts, anyway.

This chapter is your robe. Not flashy, not decorative, but earned through repetition, through miscasts and recoveries, through showing up to the page when you didn't feel like it and still writing something true.

The final spell isn't taught.
It's lived.
In the way you speak to others.
In the energy you carry into a room.
In the way you build, rest, create, teach, and forgive.

The Shift

It will look different for everyone.

For one person, the final spell might be speaking a truth they've hidden for years. For another, it might be choosing to rest after decades of self-imposed striving. For you, it might be showing up one more time with your entire self because this time, you're not pretending to be someone else. You've stopped seeking permission. You've stopped waiting for the robe to be handed to you.

You've claimed it.
You're no longer practicing your magic. You're living it.
That's the shift, and it's irreversible.

There's a moment that defines this stage, not as a lesson, but as a truth. It's the realization that the page is blank again, but this time, you aren't afraid of it. Because now you understand. Blank doesn't mean empty. It means potential. It means invitation. It means you get to write the spell only *you* could write.

You've stopped asking, *What spell am I missing?*
You've started asking, *What Wizard have I already become?*
Mastery no longer lives in reaching. It lives in rhythm.

The Grimoire Lives

Your life is no longer a student's notebook. It's a grimoire now.

A living record of what you've seen, what you've tried, what you've failed, what you've survived, and what you're choosing to shape. You're not here to collect spells anymore. You're here to leave them behind for the ones who come next.

This is the part of the journey where your questions become doors for others to walk through. Where your choices become teaching tools. Where your voice starts to carry, not because you're trying to be heard, but because it's grounded in something real.

You don't need to memorize everything you've learned here. You don't need to recite the spells you've cast. You just need to trust that it's in you now and that when the moment comes, you'll know exactly what to say, what to build, what to hold.

Because you've done the work.
You've lived the practice.
And now, you live the page.

The Archmage Edict

This isn't a prompt or a challenge. It's a declaration. A remembering.

Write your edict, not to impress, but to anchor. One line. One truth. One spell that will stay with you long after this book is finished.

It could be:

I cast slow magic.
I speak only from the truth.
I do not rush my remembering.
I leave light behind.
I show up softly and still change everything.

Whatever it is, make it yours. Whisper it if needed. Carry it if you must. Write it where it can be seen.

Not to be perfect.

To be present.

You don't need to cling to the page anymore. The magic isn't just in what you've read, it's in how you live now. You're not just following the path. You're carrying it forward.

And that… is the final spell.

The Grimoire Remains

"The spell fades. The Wizard ages. But the mark remains, in margin notes, in memories, in the ones who kept reading."
— *The Unknown Archmage*

What Remains

You won't always be here. But something you've made will be.

That realization comes slowly for most Wizards. Early on, we think magic is about immediate change, cast a spell, feel the result, but with time and practice, you understand that some of the most powerful magic isn't about what happens in the moment. It's about what lasts. It's about what's still there, long after the wand is set down, the candles burn out, and the circle is erased. That's what the grimoire holds. Not just the spells you've cast, but the ones that keep working in your absence.

And here's the secret: you've been writing your grimoire all along. Every time you returned to your practice instead of giving up, every time you chose reflection over reaction, every time you made something with intention, those moments became ink. You don't have to publish it or bind it, or even share it. But it exists. The trace is real.

This chapter is not about documentation for the sake of legacy. It's about what happens when you begin to live in such a way that your presence remains after you leave a space. The Wizard's grimoire isn't necessarily a physical book. It's everything you've lived that someone else might one day find meaningful. And most of the time, you won't get to know which pieces mattered. That's not the point. The point is to live as though they *could*.

Why I'm Writing This

I didn't begin this series with the idea of legacy. I didn't picture someone reading it years from now, holding it with reverence or awe. I started writing because I was trying to survive the weight of remembering everything on my own.

I had scraps of language that grounded me, phrases I'd collected from other teachers and from my own hard-earned clarity. There were notes written in the margins of notebooks, thoughts scratched onto napkins, things I muttered to myself on bad days because I couldn't afford to forget them. These weren't lessons. They were lifelines.

Eventually, I realized I was carrying a scattered grimoire, even if I hadn't called it that yet. And if it helped me remember how to show up as myself, it might help someone else. That was the beginning of this book. Not a teaching plan. A trail of breadcrumbs. A signal flare. A door left slightly ajar for the next person looking for a way through.

I wrote this for the version of me who didn't know you could live this way. For the one who assumed a life of presence, rhythm, and quiet power belonged to other people, people with more discipline, more support, more clarity. I wrote it for the person who always felt slightly out of step with the world and needed a different tempo. I wrote it because I wished someone had written it for me.

Now that it exists, I can see it for what it is. This is my grimoire. Not a manual, not a manifesto. Just a record of what I've lived and what I chose to remember. If something here stays with you, if something here becomes part of your own spellwork, then I've left something behind that matters.

The Legacy We Don't See

We all want to believe that the work we do has meaning, but it's easy to forget that most of our impact won't come from the moments we plan. Legacy is rarely visible in the moment it's created. More often, it lives quietly in the background, unnoticed until someone else stumbles across it, years later, and realizes they needed exactly that piece of light.

I remember a moment when someone quoted one of my lines back to me in conversation. They didn't know I had written it. They had heard it secondhand, maybe passed through another person or embedded in something someone else had shared. It had taken root somewhere and continued to live without needing my name attached.

That moment changed something for me. It wasn't about being proud. It was about realizing that my magic had moved beyond me. That it could ripple, shift, and soften someone else's experience without me ever knowing. That is the nature of the grimoire, not a monument to be admired, but a tool to be used.

You won't always get to see what you've left behind. But you can trust that something remains. When you cast with care, when you live with presence, when you speak your truth without needing attention, those things echo. Not loudly, but deeply.

You don't need to see the legacy in order to believe in it.

One Page Is Enough

Not everything you create has to change the world. Sometimes, a single line is enough. A sentence written in a journal that your future self stumbles across when they most need it. A story shared with a friend that gives them the courage to begin again. A truth spoken, softly, that shifts the entire room.

The grimoire is not a volume of perfect insight. It's a record of presence. What matters is not how much you leave, but whether you left *something*. Something that could be found, picked up, carried, remembered.

You don't need a massive following. You don't need a published book or a platform. You just need to believe that the way you live matters enough to be remembered. That the decisions you make in small moments, when no one's watching, can carry forward in ways you'll never fully know.

So let this be the invitation. Choose one piece of your story. One piece of your truth. One thing that helped you make it through. And write it down. Not for performance. Not for applause. Just so that it exists in the world.

Because someone will need it. And when they find it, it will feel like a spell.

The Archmage Edict

This is not a summary. It is a choice.

Write a single line that belongs in your grimoire, not to explain who you were, but to shape who you're becoming.

A truth to live by.
A presence to carry forward.
A trace of the magic you want to leave behind.

Examples:

I teach through how I live.

I leave behind light, even when I'm tired.

I trust the trace I'm leaving is enough.

I cast spells in silence and still believe they work.

I'm building something that may outlast me.

Make it yours. Make it real. Then let it remain.

Wizards Never Retire

> *"A Wizard is not someone who finishes the path. A Wizard is someone who keeps returning to it."*
> — The Unknown Archmage

The Long View

There are moments, quiet and unremarkable on the surface, where something in you finally understands: you are not going back. Not to the old ways of being, not to the disconnection, not to the life lived on autopilot. The moment doesn't arrive with thunder or applause. It often comes after silence, or rest, or a long walk. But it comes.

By the time you arrive here, this far into the practice, this deep into the remembering, your magic no longer lives in performance. It lives in presence. The work isn't about becoming something new anymore. It's about remaining what you are.

This chapter is not a last lesson. It's a long, steady breath at the end of a long walk. Not because the journey is over, but because you've earned a moment to pause, to look back, and to quietly recognize what you've become.

Wizards never retire because there's no exit from the path. Not because it traps you, but because it becomes part of you. Magic is no longer something you do. It's how you move. How you meet yourself. How you return.

The Circle, Not the Line

At the beginning of this book, the path may have looked like a straight line, pointing toward mastery, or clarity, or control. But by now, you know it better. You know it loops. Doubles back. Spirals and folds and pulls you into the same lessons again, each time from a different vantage.

This isn't a failure of progress. It's the shape of the work. It teaches you that growth isn't a march. It's a deepening. What once felt like starting over is now understood as returning, wiser, slower, more grounded.

You've likely walked away from your magic at some point. Maybe more than once. You've forgotten what worked. You've slipped back into habits that don't serve you. And yet, you're here. Still casting. Still returning. That's not weakness. That's the sign of a true Wizard. The practice was never about staying on fire. It was always about coming back.

The Robe You Already Wear

The longer you walk this path, the more invisible the magic becomes, not because it's gone, but because it's integrated. The rituals don't need ceremony. The spells don't need words. The robe doesn't need to be put on in the morning. You are wearing it already.

There was a time when everything felt new, mystical, unfamiliar. But mastery is quiet. It's the moment you hold a boundary without drama. It's when you speak softly and still shake the room. It's when you let go of a need to prove that you're a Wizard, because you've stopped doubting it.

This is not about confidence. It's about continuity.

The robe doesn't wear out. It evolves with you.
You're not casting to become someone anymore.
You're casting to remain who you are.

What You Leave Behind

At this stage, you may feel like there's less urgency to learn something new. That's natural. The work begins to shift from inward excavation to outward expression. You begin to see that your life is the grimoire now. You're not trying to hold on to magic. You're releasing it. Into conversations, into spaces, into the choices no one sees but everyone feels.

You've already changed more than you know. You've left spells behind, spoken or unspoken, that someone else may carry without realizing their origin. That is the quiet transmission of this path. Wizards don't retire because there is always someone watching. Listening. Waiting for permission to live with intention. You won't know when they hear you. You don't need to.

Sometimes magic works long after the caster has moved on.

The Myth of Retirement

Retirement is a concept built around jobs. Tasks. Outcomes. But this isn't a job. It's not a title you put down, or a season you finish. A Wizard doesn't retire because being a Wizard isn't something you do. It's something you become.

And once you've become it, even if you stop writing, even if you stop casting in obvious ways, even if you go quiet, you're still shaping the space around you. You still hold the charge.

There will be days when you feel far from your practice. There will be long stretches where nothing seems to work. The spells falter. The spark feels gone. But in those moments, you won't forget yourself the way you used to. You've come too far for that.

This is what staying means. Not always performing. Not always growing. Just staying.

Even if only in your own presence.

The Unknown Archmage

The Unknown Archmage has spoken throughout these pages. Some of their words were found in scrolls. Others on stone, in song, in the margins of books long lost.

I've quoted them faithfully. Or as faithfully as memory allows.

Some say the Archmage was one person. Others say they were many. A mask. A lineage. A voice that appears when needed. What matters is that the words remain. And maybe now, if you've read this far, you understand why.

Maybe you've started to hear your own voice in theirs.

The Archmage Edict

You've written your share of spells. You've drawn your circles. You've passed the point of seeking and arrived at something deeper.

This final edict is not a goal. It's a reflection of who you've become.

Write a single line you'll carry forward, not as a task, but as a truth.

- I no longer search for the path. I walk it.

- I teach with no need to be seen.
- My robe is quiet, but my presence is lasting.
- I speak from the still center now.
- I stay.

Let it be the one thing that remains, even when all else is quiet.

Because Wizards never retire. They simply take their place at the edge of the circle, and hold the light until the next one arrives.

Becoming the Archmage

You've reached a threshold few do. You've stayed with the work. You've returned. And somewhere along the way, you stopped asking if you were worthy of the robe.

You simply wore it.

The robe no longer belongs to someone else. It belongs to you. You are the one who returns. You are the one who carries the map. You are the one whose words will echo.

Whether you choose to claim the title or not, you've stepped into the mantle.

You are the Archmage now.

And when the next class begins, you'll be there. Not at the front. But in the echoes. In the notes. In the spells that continue to live. Just like the ones you found here.

The Next Class Begins

You may not feel ready to pass anything on. Most Wizards don't. And yet, here you are, holding a kind of light you didn't have when you began. Not the blinding kind. Not the stage light. The firelight. The kind you sit beside. The kind you offer to others when the wind gets cold, and the world gets loud.

You've done the work. You've lived the pages. You've remembered who you are and forgotten and remembered again. That's the magic. Not that it stayed easy, but that you stayed with it.

And now, someone else is picking up the book for the first time.

They don't know the spells yet. They don't know the shape of the robe, or the difference between rest and quitting, or why drawing a circle before casting matters so much. But they'll learn, because you did, and whether you meet them or not, your presence will be there. In the way, the words resonate. In the way, the space you helped hold remains open. In the fact that they found this book at all.

This is how the work continues.

Quietly.
Relationally.
Without credit or applause.
One reader at a time.
One return at a time.

The next class is arriving. Not all at once, and not with trumpets. Just with a question in their chest, and a book in their hand.

Just like you once did.

You are not done, but you're not at the beginning anymore, either. You're in the part of the story where you begin to witness. Where you see others take their first steps and remember how hard and beautiful those first steps were.

You don't have to teach them.

You just have to stay lit. Stay real. Stay visible in the ways that matter. Because someone, somewhere, is deciding right now whether they're allowed to live a life like this. And your existence may be the answer.

There will be other books.
Other teachers.
Other spells.

This one was yours, this chapter, this journey, this robe, and you wore it well. You cast when you could. You returned when you couldn't. You shaped something lasting. You left light behind. So let this be your final gesture:

Leave the circle open.
Not for applause.

Not for legacy.

Just in case someone else is looking for it.

> "The Wizard who helped you may never know your name. But the
> one you help might never forget it."
> — *Scroll Fragment 51c, inscribed in ash and gold*

Thank you for walking this path.
Thank you for remembering.
Thank you for casting.

Class is not dismissed. It's just beginning. And this time, you're at the edge
of the circle.

Welcome, Archmage. We're ready for the next class.

> ***"Let them teach spells. We'll teach survival."***
> — *The Whisper from the Shadows*

Another path is open. Some find it first. Others find it when they're ready.

The Rogue is waiting.

The Wizards Codex

You don't need to play D&D or read fantasy novels to get this. These terms are metaphors, shortcuts to deeper ideas about learning, growth, and change. Here's what they really mean:

Spell - A focused action with intent. In this world, a spell is anything you do deliberately to learn, grow, or shift reality. Writing a journal entry, asking a good question, or finishing a hard task? That's spellcasting. *(See also: Casting)*

Spellbook - Your personal record of growth. A journal, a Notion page, a notebook, whatever holds your thoughts, reflections, and insights. This is where your evolution lives.

Ritual - A small, meaningful routine that brings focus. Lighting a candle before writing. A breath before work. A question before committing. It's not about being fancy, it's about being present.

Casting - Taking action. Showing up. A spell isn't cast when it's perfect, it's cast when it's *done with intent. (See also: Spell, Ritual)*

Mana - Your energy. Mental, emotional, creative. Mana isn't infinite, it runs low. Managing your mana means knowing your limits and resting when needed. *(Think: your internal battery.)*

Archmage - A future version of you. Experienced, steady, still learning. Also: anyone who's walked this path long enough to guide others with wisdom, not ego.

Circle - A boundary you draw to focus. The moment before the work begins. A pause. A signal to yourself: "This matters." (*See also: Preparation, Ritual*)

Focus - Your mental attention. The "wand" that directs your energy. Without focus, your power scatters. With it, you can shape reality.

Wand - Whatever helps you focus your energy. Could be a pen, a laptop, a whiteboard, or a quiet room. The object is symbolic, the real power is in you.

Scroll - A reference source. Books, saved notes, highlights, resources, scrolls are how you learn from the magic others have already discovered.

Tower - Not a place. A mindset. Your personal space for deep work, solitude, and perspective. Your "tower" could be your desk, your routine, or your walk around the block.

Grimoire - A deeper version of your spellbook. Less about notes, more about transformation. Where you keep the lessons, stories, and breakthroughs that change you.

Class - The role or growth path you choose. Wizard is just one. Others (like Bard or Paladin) represent other archetypes, ways of moving through the world.

Multiclass - Blending strengths from more than one path. You can be a Wizard with Bard energy. A Monk who knows how to perform. No one's one thing.

Apprentice - You, at the beginning. Curious, messy, brave. Not less than just early.

Novice - You, in motion. Still learning, but with rhythm. A little steadier. A little more sure. This is where your magic gains momentum.

Arcane - Things that are deep, mysterious, or layered. Arcane knowledge isn't hidden, it just takes patience and curiosity to understand.

Incantation - Words you repeat to anchor yourself. A mantra, a creed, a line that reminds you of who you are becoming.

Burnout - When you cast too many spells without resting. Not failure. Just a sign that your mana is spent, and it's time to restore.

Cantrip - A tiny, low-effort action that still builds magic over time. Think of these as your daily rituals, quick, repeatable, and powerful. *(See also: Ritual)*

Prep - The work before the work. Laying things out. Making space. Creating the mental or physical conditions that help your future self succeed.

Beginner's Magic - The power of being new. You're free to ask big questions and try bold ideas because you don't yet know the "rules." That's a gift.

Ritual Casting - When a practice becomes a rhythm. Not just a routine, but something you return to with purpose, because it keeps you grounded.

Mana Management - The art of knowing when to push and when to rest. Great Wizards don't just work hard, they recover well.

Alchemy - Turning learning into transformation. Not just knowing something, but using it to reshape how you live. That's the real magic.

Acknowledgements

This book was written slowly.

Not in a tower, but in the quiet in-between spaces. Between work and rest, between memory and imagination, between who I was and who I was becoming. It arrived in fragments, in the middle of conversations, in old notebooks and whispered truths I wasn't ready to speak out loud yet. It's a record of remembering. A long spell cast one line at a time.

To my wife — thank you for being the stillness in the noise. The grounding in the myth. You made space for this, again and again, and I'll never stop being grateful for it.

To my daughter — you are the light I want to leave behind. Every spell I've written carries a trace of the world I hope you get to live in. One where magic is real, softness is strength, and every version of yourself is welcome.

To my brother and sister — Jimmy and Star — thank you for being part of the magic long before it had a name. You've always been part of this circle.

To my mom — though you're no longer here, thank you for the belief, the encouragement, and the space to explore who I was becoming. You helped build the foundation I still return to.

To my friends — Alexa, Shelly, Zac, Logan, Ken, Michael M, and Michael G — you've helped shape this book more than you know. Through ideas, through conversations, through moments where the spark dimmed, and you helped me find it again. Thank you for seeing the Wizard in me, even when I didn't.

And finally, to the reader.

This book is for you. For those who always felt a little out of step. For the seeker. For the one who quietly suspected there was another way to live, one with meaning, rhythm, magic, and return. If you found a page that stayed with you, then I've done what I came to do.

May your robe never fade.
May your circle remain open.
And may the next spell you cast bring you home.

About the Author

Todd Campbell is a writer, analyst, and architect of quiet magic.

He believes that wonder is a skill, that intention shapes reality, and that even the smallest rituals can bring us back to who we truly are. This book is part of his living grimoire, a spell long in the making, written not in theory, but in practice.

Todd lives between the world that is and the one he's still building, one where Wizards return to themselves, Rogues rewrite the rules, and everyone is invited to walk their own path with power and presence.

He still writes most of his spells by hand.

You can connect with me on:
- https://www.toddtheauthor.com
- https://linktr.ee/Todd_The_Author